CHAOS COME AGAIN

LION'S ZOO
BOOK ONE

JUDE KNIGHT

TITCHFIELD
PRESS

CHAOS COME AGAIN

Nothing will stop Colonel Lionel O'Toole from leading his men on the invasion into Spain. Not the abducted heiress he rescues and makes his wife, nor old secrets that radically change his place in his family, nor the ill health of the earl his grandfather.

But his devotion to duty might be derailed by the spy in his inner circle and scandal surrounding his wife.

Will the love between Lion and Dorothea endure, or will deceit and betrayal tear them apart?

Tormented by his past and by vile rumours, will this Regency Othello allow a trusted liar to destroy the love between himself and his wife?

CHAPTER 1

N *orth Yorkshire, 1st of May, 1813*

When Roderick Westinghouse locked Dorothea Brabant in the tiny box of a room, he said he would return shortly with food and drink. She immediately tried the window, but it was nailed shut. In any case, they had come up flight after flight of stairs to reach the attic room. It was normally occupied by three maids, the landlord explained, who would tonight be sleeping in the kitchen. From the window, Dorothea could see a sheer drop to the cobbled stable yard, slick in the driving rain.

She glared at the bag full of her own clothes that Roderick had dumped just inside the door. Someone in her own home had betrayed her, and she was certain she knew whom.

After she changed her damp stockings and outerwear as quickly as she could, she stood where she would be hidden by the opening door, the chamber pot held high. It was the only portable item in the room heavy enough to knock Roderick Westinghouse out when he returned to the bedchamber.

Her arms grew too tired to maintain the position, so she let them down, but still she remained by the door for what seemed like hours. She was hungry and thirsty, and she wanted to use the chamber pot for its proper purpose, but she would have only one chance against her abductor. She could not afford to be caught without her weapon at the ready.

She should not be surprised Roderick forgot to feed her. One of the reasons she'd given her father for refusing the man's proposal was his preference for his male drinking companions, for whom he would desert her without notice, leaving her unattended at whatever event her father had insisted on her attending with the man.

One reason among many. Roderick was seldom sober. He was addicted to sport—or, rather, to gambling on sport. In fact, he would gamble on anything and Dorothea was certain her chief attraction to him was the access their marriage would give him to her father's deep pockets.

Not the only attraction. His gaze on her feminine assets made her feel dirty, but he would not have courted her for that alone. He made no bones about examining every attractive female of whatever status with the same lecherous eyes, and she knew—for the unkind gossips had made certain she heard—that he had had at least one mistress at a time in his keeping until his money ran out.

Papa said such behaviour was to be expected of the son of an earl, and her compensation would be the eventual title of countess. Papa had done his research, and was certain that Roderick's brother would not have sons, though Dorothea had no idea how he could be so sure and he would not explain.

Being a countess would be no compensation, Dorothea thought. She had watched her dear friend Agnes suffer after she married a man who was a gentleman in public and a brute in private. Roderick was not even a gentleman in public.

The inn settled as the night drew on. The lamps went out one by one—those in the stable across the courtyard and the reflected light from those in the inn. She no longer heard sounds from the rooms around her and those immediately below. Even the drunken singing that sailed up through the floors from the public room settled as one voice after another fell silent.

Roderick didn't come.

She was almost asleep, leaning against the wall, the chamber pot dangling from one hand when she heard the key striking against the metal of the lock as someone on the other side made several attempts to insert it.

Wide awake, her heart racing, she raised the chamber pot, and just in time, as the key finally slid into the lock and turned, and the door opened. Roderick stumbled into the room, stopped to gape at the bed, and crumpled to the ground as Dorothea brought the chamber pot down on the back of his head.

For a moment, she feared she had hit him too hard, but he groaned, so she grabbed her bag and flung herself out of the room. He had left the key in the lock, so she turned it, standing for a moment in fear he would start shouting and banging. Instead, heavy snoring rumbled through the door.

Dorothea stayed no longer, but ran to the other end of the passage that ran the length of the house, and crept quietly down the stairs.

During her long wait, she'd had time to plan her next move. She would not throw herself on the mercy of the innkeeper. Roderick had not only insisted she was his wife, he had explained she was feeble-minded after the death of a child, and he was taking her to Edinburgh for medical care. "She denies she is even my wife," he had told the innkeeper, with tears in his eyes. "I can only pray they can do something to help her."

No. The innkeeper would only hand her back to Roderick, as would anyone in the village. She found the door to the stable yard. It was not locked, thank goodness, and no one was about.

She had seen a carriage arrive late in the afternoon that was perfect for her needs.

She crossed the wet cobbles, hunched against the persistent drizzle, grateful for a single lantern in a glass cover that was affixed to one of the walls. First, she must find a dark corner in which to relieve herself. Through a little gate was a small garden, which would have to do. Once she was more comfortable, she crept into the carriage house, quietly, in case someone was there.

A covered lamp in the carriage house gave off a dim light. No one was inside, and she could see the vehicle she remembered. One of the two men who had ridden inside had carried two large soft bags from the carriage, but had not opened the storage box under the groom's seat on the back.

She opened the hatch that gave access to the box. It contained a trunk, and another couple of bags, all near the opening to the compartment for easy access. She leaned forward into the shadows behind them. As far as she could tell, it was empty.

Dorothea pushed her own bag across the back of the trunk until it fell into the space, then wriggled over the other bags. It was a tight fit, and she had no way to shut the hatch, but she should be completely hidden from view. Better still, she had her bag to rest her head on, and she was lying on what felt like carriage blankets.

A bit more wriggling, and she was wrapped, warm and cosy, in the blankets. They were even pleasantly scented with some sort of herb. Rosemary, she thought. In moments, she was asleep.

She woke, momentarily disoriented, when someone slammed the hatch. *My bedchamber door?* The sound was wrong, the bed was unaccountably hard, and she was jammed between two hard walls.

Ah, yes. She had escaped from the loathsome Roderick and was hidden in a luggage box behind a stranger's carriage. She held very still and very silent as the coach rocked, bounced, and then stilled again. Were they putting the horses to the traces? Yes. She could hear men talking.

"Early start," said one.

"It is at that," said another. "The colonel has a long way to go today."

"At least he feeds us well," commented another. "Polite, too."

"He's a good officer," the second man said, his tone edged with belligerence, as if he expected opposition.

One of the others changed the subject. "At least it isn't raining. Looks fair to the north, too."

"Sir!" That barked greeting was the second man.

A new voice replied in crisp aristocratic tones. From the sound, he was only a few feet away from her. "Stand easy, corporal. You've all eaten, men? Good. Are we ready to go?"

He must have received an affirmative to both of his questions, because the carriage rocked as the men climbed into their places. She remembered a groom, a driver, and two occupants. The colonel and the corporal, presumably.

It was the colonel she heard next, his deep rumble just on the other side of the wall between her and the coach interior. "Chequers, Blythe?"

The horses got into their stride, and the vehicle settled to a rocking motion with the occasional lurch as the wheels bounced on a hole or a rut. Dorothea drifted off to sleep again to the sound of the two men talking.

C olonel Lionel O'Toole entered the carriage for the fifth morning in a row, leaving his soldier servant to put up the steps and clamber in after him.

"Chequers, Blythe?" he asked. The corporal nodded and pulled out a folding wooden box, opening it and setting out the pieces, pegging each in place. The board was marked on the inside base; alternate squares of ebony and ash, each with a central hole for a peg.

Blythe had a well-deserved reputation as a chequers champion, and Lion had to concentrate to win a respectable share of their matches, which at least passed the time.

"At least the rain is holding off today, colonel," Blythe commented.

"Yes," Lion agreed. "That will make travel easier." Blythe's approach to life was one of counting blessings. Lion privately thought this trip offered far too few of them. He shouldn't be here at all. He should be in Portugal with his men, preparing for the summer offensive into Spain.

Instead, his grandfather had sent for him. Him and his cousin Fox. Through the Marquess of Wellington, so that Lion was not given the opportunity to ignore the summons. Years of practice had brought Lion's volatile temper under iron control.

His voice held nothing of his resentment at his grandfather's manipulations. "I wonder if Major Foxton has passed us somehow and will be at Persham Abbey before us." Fox, unlike Lion, was dependent on the earl's allowance.

"The major did not seem to see any need to hurry," said Blythe, diplomatically. "Unless he followed no more than two hours after we left and passed us when we stopped to repair the axle pins, we've gone as fast as the coach and horses could travel."

True. As fast as the execrable weather allowed. And it was unlikely Fox had been in a hurry to leave the game pullet he'd been with in London. Fox would talk his way out of trouble, no doubt. "We'll see. We will probably arrive at Pershaw Abbey some time tomorrow."

The second of May, which would be a day after the deadline in the Earl of Ruthford's summons. His grandfather would not be pleased, but what was new? His lordship had only rarely been pleased with Lion since the day the boy arrived on his doorstep, having left behind in India the graves of his mother, his father, and his O'Toole grandfather.

The earl had taken Lion in, housed him, had him educated, bought him a commission in the army, even occasionally deigned to notice him. But Lion had always known that the man was disappointed in his heir's only offspring. Lion could do nothing to change that. He was illegitimate, which was bad enough. He was also the son of a part-Indian, part-Irish mother, which was worse.

His mind drifted to his cousin Fox again. Fox was the son of Lion's aunt, the earl's only daughter, and something of a favourite with the earl. Fox's friendly nature and ready charm made him a favourite with everyone. Except, perhaps, his mother and his elder brother.

They were the same age. Lion's temper and his fists had won him a grudging respect at school, but he owed his eventual acceptance to the ready friendship Fox had offered from the first day they met.

Blythe's voice interrupted his reverie. "Another game, sir?"

Blythe had jumped and collected his last three pieces in one move. His distraction had cost him the game.

"I'm afraid I am no match for you this morning, Blythe. I'll work for a while, I think." *And see if I can pay more attention to my correspondence than I did to chequers.*

The corporal pulled out the book that he carried in his pocket and Lion opened his documents satchel. He had to respond to reports from the managers who looked after the investments he'd purchased over the years with his prize money and the miserly allowance his grandfather continued to pay, mostly so the old man could threaten to remove it whenever Lion displeased him.

Which was not so often these days. Lion saw little of the earl, and kept his tongue between his teeth when he did see him. Once again, he wondered why the earl had sent for him. *He didn't want me and Fox back for the funerals of my uncle Harry and Harry's son Matthew. Why now?*

He had thrived in the army, though he was inclined to put that down at least in part to the gruesome winnowing of senior officers. However it might be, his scandalous origins had not kept him from becoming one of the youngest colonels in Britain's army.

Once he no longer needed the earl's allowance to keep a horse under him and a uniform on his back, Lion's pride urged him to reject the money. The hurt boy in him reckoned the earl owed him some recompense for the misery of the years under the old man's thumb after his other grandfather sent him to England.

His common sense pointed out that the earl paid allowances to all his children's offspring, regular and irregular, though those who had been born on the right side of the blanket, like Fox, received double what was paid to the bastards.

Perhaps Lion was better off than Fox at that. He had been forced to abstemious habits that meant he was better able to handle his income once he had one large enough to require handling. Fox, even now, spent his officer's pay and his quarterly allowance to the hilt, as soon as the money arrived. Prize money evaporated in the heat haze of women, gambling, and alcohol. Every quarter, Fox spent the last few weeks grumbling that he was on the rocks. He never seemed to learn.

By the first change, Lion had written notes for three replies. He'd write out fair copies when they were not moving. The next stage should bring them to Northallerton, and between here and there, he might as well read his own book, a recently published English translation of a Roman manuscript history of Alexander the Great.

As they pulled into an inn courtyard, Lion felt under his seat for his bag. *Not there.* Blythe must have loaded it in the baggage. "Blythe," he said, "When you have a moment while we're stopped, please retrieve my book from my bag."

He was several steps across the courtyard on his way to collect a couple of jugs of ale for him and his men when he heard Blythe shout. "Colonel, come here! There's someone in the luggage box."

CHAPTER 2

Blythe was not the excitable sort, but he had his hand on the knife in his belt. Lion strode to his side and peered into the box. Sure enough, when the corporal had removed Lion's bag to retrieve the book Lion wanted, the space behind it proved to have something in it. A neat little foot shod in a half boot had been poking out of one of the spare carriage rugs, but shifted as Lion watched, retreating into cover.

"Too late," Lion told the hidden woman. "Come on out, or we shall remove the luggage and drag you out."

Silence, and then the woman spoke. "Would you be good enough to remove at least the other bag? I managed to get in, head first, but I do not seem to have enough room to back out." She was making a praiseworthy attempt at remaining calm, but a slight quaver hinted at fear.

Wise woman. Lion was not minded to forgive her trespass—and the delay it might cause—unless she had a very good reason for it. Wise lady, rather. That was not the accent of a barmaid or a farmgirl.

He gave the corporal a nod, and they took one side of the trunk each, hefting it from the box.

Their stowaway emerged, struggling at first to remove the blanket in which she had wrapped herself, then crawling into the space he and Blythe had made. Behind her, he could see the shape of a bag that was not his. The lady's, he assumed.

She sat up, her brow creased as she calculated how to get out of the box. Small as she was, her options were limited. She could make a dive head first, but the box was at least thirty inches above the ground, and the base of the hatch eighteen inches higher still. If she managed to get her behind on the edge of the hatch, she might be able to swing her legs over, but she was likely to expose more than she might be comfortable with.

He resolved her conundrum by reaching in, grasping her waist, and lifting her out through the hatch. She was as light as a feather, and his hands nearly spanned the tiny waist. She let out a yelp of surprise as he set her on her feet, having successfully resisted the temptation to slide her down his body.

"Thank you for your help," she said, as politely as if he had just fetched her a glass of punch or assisted her to step over a puddle. Definitely a lady. *So, what on earth is a lady doing hiding in my luggage box?*

That really wasn't the important question. *What am I going to do with her?*

Lion needed more information, and he intended to get it. Courtesy might work. It was certainly a place to start. "I am Colonel O'Toole, and this is Corporal Blythe. May I know the name of the lady I have been honoured to assist?"

She curtseyed. There in the muddy courtyard of a dirty country inn, with her hair tumbling down and her clothes grubby, creased and crumpled, she curtseyed like a princess at a London ball. "Miss Dorothea Brabant, and I really am most awfully grateful."

"Cor," said the groom. "She's a lady."

Lion looked around to see that they had an audience. Not just his groom and driver, but several ostlers and a couple of locals, gazing with interest from Lion to Miss Brabant and back again.

"Walk the horses," he ordered the groom. "Corporal, fetch Miss Brabant's bag and organise some washing water and a maid to assist the lady. Miss Brabant?" He offered his arm. She took it, wide eyed, and he escorted her into the inn, where they were met by the innkeeper's wife."

"Here!" She challenged them. "I'll have no wicked goings on at my inn!"

Miss Brabant's hand trembled on his arm.

"My sister will require a room in which to wash and change," Lion stated, firmly.

"She ent no sister," the innkeeper's wife sneered. He didn't expect her to believe him. After all, her servants had seen him introduce himself to the woman. He did expect her to pretend to accept his statement and obey his instructions.

Lion raised his eyebrows and glared. The woman quailed, and her husband said, "No harm in washing, Lilly."

Blythe, bless him, arrived with the lady's bag and a bucket of water, a maid following behind him with a towel tucked under one arm. "Water and maid, colonel," he reported.

Lion held up a crown, and the innkeeper's wife folded. "First door at the top of the stairs," she told the maid, who led the procession of Blythe, Lion and Miss Brabant up two flights of stairs, followed by the innkeeper's wife. At the top, the maid opened a door to a bedchamber.

Lion waited outside as Blythe put the bag on the bed and the bucket next to the washstand before retreating into the passage. Under the suspicious gaze of the innkeeper's wife, Miss Brabant slipped her hand from Lion's arm. "Thank you, brother. I shall be as fast as I can."

"And then we shall be on our way to Northallerton, and you shall explain to me how and why you came to be here," he promised. Her eyes widened, but she bobbed him a curtsey and entered the room, where the maid and all that she needed for her comfort, he hoped, awaited her.

No. Perhaps not quite all. "My sister will require something to eat and something to drink," he told the innkeeper's wife. "Something we can take with us, as we are already losing time thanks to this foolish start of hers. Also, a jug of ale and four tumblers." The men were probably thirsty, and might as well have something to drink while they waited.

Silently, she held out her hand. He put a florin in it, and followed her downstairs. He ordered a mug of tea to be delivered when Miss Brabant rejoined him, and went outside with a small basket of food—three pence extra for the basket, and six pence for the mug, which was highway robbery, but he was in no mood to haggle.

"Are we taking her with us, then, Colonel?" Blythe asked him.

Lion shrugged. "We cannot leave her here." *In a small inn on a major highway, unprotected.* He was certain she needed protection. He had met many harpies and more adventuresses, especially as his rank and wealth grew. He'd even proposed marriage to one and thought his heart broken, until he discovered her true nature.

All his instincts said Miss Brabant was not such a two-faced cheat. It was only fair to hear her out. Besides, he wanted to know why she had hidden away in his carriage.

Blythe accepted his decree without comment.

The new horses were in the traces, and the groom was walking them while he waited. Lion watched the carriage make another circuit of the stable yard and suppressed a sigh. A short delay here. Another delay once he discovered Miss Brabant's story and discovered somewhere safe to leave her. He could still be at Persham Abbey tomorrow, only a day late.

Dammit. Where is Fox? I could do with him now. Perhaps he had gone another way. Perhaps he had decided not to go at all, although his dependence on the earl's allowance argued against that.

Lion wanted to get the visit over and done, and return to his men in Portugal. Not that Michael Cassiday wasn't very capable, but Lion should be there, dammit.

🐫🐫🐫🐫🐪

Dorothea had woken with a start when the corporal had opened the box and started shouting. After that, she'd been given no time to find her balance as Colonel O'Toole gave his orders to her, his corporal, and the staff of the inn.

Everyone fell in with his wishes. She supposed she should be grateful that he seemed inclined to help her. In return for her story, it would appear.

She was going to have to tell him. After all, what choice did she have? Whoever had packed a bag for her had included no cash and nothing she could sell. She should have searched Roderick and taken his money, but she had not thought of it. If Colonel O'Toole would not assist her, she would be alone and penniless in a strange village far from home.

If he did help, what price would he demand? Dorothea had been raised to fear being alone with a man; warned of nameless and disastrous things that would leave her fit for nothing but the streets. Her experiences with Roderick had given some shape to those formless fears. She shuddered at the memories.

Colonel O'Toole did not make her shudder. Shiver, perhaps. When he had picked her up from the luggage box, she had felt not frightened but safe. He was, after all, a senior officer in His Majesty's army. Surely, he could be trusted?

She washed quickly and changed from the skin out. The maid helped with her stays, and with buttoning her blue carriage gown, the only other dress she had. She turned the gown she had been wearing inside out and rolled the rest of her dirty clothes in it to put them in the bag.

"Just something simple," she told the maid who was fussing with her hair. "The colonel is anxious to be on his way."

"He is a powerful handsome man," the maid commented. "Doesn't look much like you, miss."

"We have different mothers," Dorothea said. *A lie wrapped up in a truth.*

The maid's reflection showed her opinion of that—a saucy smirk. "Powerful handsome," she repeated.

Dorothea had to agree. He was very handsome. Powerful, too, as she had reason to know. Close cropped black hair, heavy black eyebrows over dark eyes, skin tanned brown, or perhaps brown by nature. A Spanish or Italian mother or grandmother, perhaps? The name suggested he was Irish, but the Irish people she had met all had very fair skin.

Meanwhile, the maid's busy fingers rolled and pinned Dorothea's hair until it was both tidy and attractive. It was a pity to cover it with her bonnet, but propriety had its own demands, even for anonymous females who had been discovered in a gentleman's luggage box and were suspected of improper intentions. Perhaps especially for such females.

Fortunately, Dorothea had been able to squeeze the bonnet mostly back into shape. She took off the ribbon and replaced it with the ribbon that that matched the gown. Arranged carefully, it covered the worst hole.

She tied the bow off to one side, and picked up her bag. "Thank you for your help. You have done exceedingly well." The girl should have a reward, but thanks would have to do, for Dorothea had nothing to give her. *No! Wait!* She put the bag back on the bed and opened it to take out the ribbon she had removed from the bonnet. "I would like to make you a gift of this as a token of my appreciation," she said.

The maid's broad grin showed her delight. "Well, now, miss. That is right nice of you."

As Dorothea did the bag back up again, the maid added. "Don't know what you're doing with the officer, miss, but you are a real lady, whatever her downstairs thinks. You be careful now."

Good advice, but too late. Dorothea should never have gone for a drive yesterday with Roderick, even if her father had insisted.

As Dorothea descended to the courtyard, she allowed herself the thought she had been avoiding since Roderick first joined her in the closed carriage. *Father knew Roderick was going to abduct me.* He had almost certainly planned it himself. The bag was evidence. No one in her father's household would have packed for her without her father's orders.

Which meant she could not go back to York, or appeal to anyone in her family for help. She sighed. All she had ever wanted was a marriage with a kind man who would stand up to her father and treat her with respect. Someone within her own class, for her Seasons in London had convinced her that the kind of marriage her father wanted for her would lead to a lifetime of being looked down on and gossiped about. After this escapade, even those modest ambitions were probably hopeless.

The colonel was leaning against the wall beside the door. He straightened as she came out of the inn, and smiled. "You were quick," he said, his dark eyes approving. He signalled to the carriage and in a moment, it rolled to a stop in front of her. Corporal Blythe relieved her of her bag, Colonel O'Toole handed her up into the carriage, and the moment to flee was gone.

Though if her heart was pumping faster than usual, at least part of that was the touch of Colonel O'Toole's hand.

The colonel followed her, and took the backward facing seat opposite her, where he was joined by Corporal Blythe, who handed her a mug of tea.

Tears of gratitude welled in Dorothea's eyes. She murmured her thanks, took a sip, and let out a deep sigh. Hot, strong, and sweet. Just what she needed.

The carriage got underway and Colonel O'Toole surprised her again, producing a basket of food. "Tuck into that, Miss Brabant. I imagine you joined us during the night. You must be hungry."

"Famished," she admitted. "I have not eaten since…" she thought about it. "Not since I broke my fast yesterday morning."

She said a quick prayer of blessing and took a bite out of a bread roll stuffed with meat and sauce. Perhaps Colonel O'Toole was a villain and she was being abducted again. But if so, he was already treating her far better than Roderick had. With a mug of tea in one hand and food in the other, she couldn't find it within herself to worry.

The colonel waited patiently until she had finished, wiped her mouth on the napkin that the inn had provided, and put that and the mug in the basket. Corporal Blythe took it off her and stowed it in a little cupboard under his seat.

"Feeling better?" Colonel O'Toole asked.

Dorothea nodded. "Thank you again. I am more grateful than I can say." Best to get right on with it. "I am sure you are wondering what brings me to this pass. May I tell you?"

If he was surprised at her taking the initiative, he didn't show it. "I would be pleased to hear your story," he said, his face showing nothing more than mild interest.

She wondered what was going on behind that calm facade.

He must have thought she was hesitating, for he assured her, "You can trust Corporal Blythe. He will keep your secrets if I instruct him to do so."

Corporal Blythe nodded his agreement. "Or I can go and sit up with the groom if the lady prefers," he offered.

"I will trust you both," Dorothea decided. "After all, I could hardly be in a worse position than I was last night." She shuddered.

The colonel leaned forward and touched her hand, his eyes suddenly warm. "You are safe with us," he reminded her, and she believed him.

However, would he continue to treat her like a lady when he knew more about her? "I should start by telling you that I am the only child of Geoffrey Brabant, a mill owner of Manchester."

"Brabant Mills," he commented. "I wondered. Brabant provides the wool for our uniforms, Blythe."

Dorothea nodded. "If you say so, Colonel O'Toole. Father does not tell me anything about his work." Until he decided to take a hand in her marriage, she had not seen her father above three or four times a year.

"He had me raised as a lady, and instructed me to make a good marriage. By which he meant that he wanted his grandchild to have a title. In my first two Seasons, I disappointed him." The only aristocrats with an interest in the daughter of a man in trade, however wealthy, were the fortune hunters and the rakes. The rakes did not want marriage. And Father had no interest in what Dorothea wanted.

"My father decided to take matters into his own hands, and arranged a marriage with the highest ranking of the fortune hunters who were prepared to ignore my family connections in favour of my wealth." Without considering the man's character or consulting Dorothea.

Colonel O'Toole's voice was without inflexion when he stated, "The man was not to your taste."

"The man is perpetually drunk and a skirt chaser. He pretended to be a gentleman in front of my father. He didn't bother when he could get me alone. He assured me he was prepared to tolerate the stink of the shop for long enough to..." she could not repeat his obnoxious comments. "Well. Suffice it to say he made it clear that life as his wife would be intolerable. I told my father what he had said, and that I would not have him."

"Father insisted I give my consent." Father had her beaten and, when that didn't change her mind, he attempted to starve her into submission. She choked back a sob as she remembered.

Colonel O'Toole had taken her hands again, and his thumbs were stroking comfort into her, rising from her hands to warm her heart.

"You continued to refuse," he said. It was not a question.

She nodded, calmed enough by his ministrations to resume her story. "Eventually, he must have realised I was not going to break. He told me we were going to York, where I would have an opportunity to find an acceptable suitor."

"After several days in York, he insisted that I go driving with the man I had repeatedly refused. He said it was only polite. Even when that man arrived in a closed carriage, my father commanded me to go. He told me not to be silly; that I would be safe enough with my maid. Then we stopped before we even left the city, and my maid abandoned me. I tried to get down too, but the man prevented me, the footman shut the door, and the carriage took off at speed."

His hands tensed on hers, then resumed their stroking.

"He abducted you, and you are running from him," he said.

CHAPTER 3

Lion's words remained calm but his emotions were raging. If Miss Brabant was an actress, she was a magnificent one. He believed her story as he watched the colour coming and going in her face, her shifting emotions all displayed in her eyes and her expression: fear, anger, hurt, despair. Her hands trembled in his when she spoke of her father's reaction to her refusal to marry a suitor who revolted her. He did not miss the telling phrase, *I was not going to break*. Whatever this dainty girl had been through, she had a core of iron.

"My father must have arranged the abduction, do you not think?" She gazed straight into his eyes, hers open and confiding, a crease or two between her eyebrows as she frowned. "When we stopped to change horses, I discovered that the coach driver and groom were not my father's men, and they laughed when I appealed to them. They woke Roderick to confine me again, and when he locked me in the inn bedchamber last night, they brought me a bag of my clothes that someone must have packed for me."

"Did he hurt you?" A little of Lion's wrath leaked into his volume. He amended the tone, and went too far the other way, as he realised he had not asked the intended question. "Did he force himself upon you." That was more of a growled whisper.

Fortunately, he didn't frighten Miss Brabant. Indeed, she seemed more bewildered by the second question than the first. "I am not much hurt. A little bruised." Her blush deepened. "I tried to hit him, and then later, when I attempted to escape, the men were rough. And Rod— the man kissed me." She withdrew one of her hands and scrubbed it over her lips as if to remove any trace of the evil brute. "He put his hands all over me. He talked about things he was going to do when we got to the inn, but then he went to sleep. He was very drunk, you see. He had finished the bottle he had with him. Rum, I think."

He was almost afraid to ask, though Miss Brabant's reaction to the question suggested the worst had not happened. "And at the inn?"

"He told the innkeeper I was his wife and insane. He said I had tried to run away with another man. He said he planned to take me to Edinburgh and put me in the charge of a doctor who would treat my madness. Then he locked me in and went away to find another drink. He said he would be back with food and would then school me in what he expected of a wife." She shrugged. "I prayed he would find the drink pleasing and would forget me. Do you think God answers such prayers?"

Not in Lion's experience. "How did you get away?" he asked. It was cowardly of him to leap to the escape and pass what might have happened before. He did not want her to be forced to tell, did not want to hear, what the man had done to the poor girl. Not the ultimate offense, he thought, he hoped. He had seen women after men had done their brutal worse. One of his own men had rescued one from a howling pack of French soldiers and brought the poor woman back to camp with him when her own father rejected her. Miss Brabant was not broken, did not flinch away from his touch.

"He took a long time to return," Miss Brabant said. "I waited. I saw your carriage arrive, and be put away in the carriage house. When I heard his key in the lock, I was behind the door with the chamber pot. I hit him over the head and he fell. I took my bag, locked the door behind me, and came to hide in your luggage box. That is the whole story, really. Except I do not know what to do next."

"What is his name, Miss?" Corporal Blythe asked. "Is it Mr Westinghouse? The Honourable?"

Lion had forgotten Blythe's presence. So, apparently, had Miss Brabant, for he felt her jerk in surprise. "It is," she confirmed.

"I saw him when I took our plates and cups back to the kitchen, Colonel," Blythe told Lion. "Big man, run to seed, balding. He and some other brutes, just as drunk, were playing cards. The innkeeper had his men serving the table, because Westinghouse had…" He paused, and found some words, blushing as he said, "offended the maids."

Groped them and worse, Lion assumed.

Lion had once known an Algernon Westinghouse. An obnoxious man. The second son of an earl; a terrible officer and a bully. His men hated him. He had died in an assault, unaccountably shot in the back, as officers loathed by their men sometimes did. "Is the man a relative of the Earl of Hernware?" he asked.

"His third son," Miss Brabant confirmed. "That is why Father favours him. He expects to be earl one day, because the second son is dead and the first has only daughters and there is something wrong with his wife. But I cannot marry Roderick, Colonel O'Toole. I cannot. The things he said…" The touch of hysteria he had been expecting all along made her voice shrill.

She clamped her mouth shut, and her eyes. After a deep breath taken in through her nose and slowly trickled from her mouth, she opened her eyes again and said, "If I go back to York, I will be forced. So, I must come up with another plan."

Her courage and determination awed Lion. He wanted to fold her in his arms and promise to protect her, and at the same time stand at her side and help her fight her own battles. It was not his place. She had just been through a terrible ordeal, and she didn't need yet another man pressing his attentions.

"Do you have family you could go to, who would stand up to your father?" he asked.

"No one. There is only me, my father, and my aunt, with whom I lived until Father decided I was to marry. She will be no help. She is kind enough, but she always does what Father tells her." That adorable little crease appeared again between her brows. "I will have to find a way to support myself."

For the remainder of the drive to Northallerton, they discussed what Miss Brabant might do to survive without her father. Almost any job, she acknowledged, would require skills and a reference. Hers were the skills of a lady.

To hear her tell it, she was trained to keep house, but not to do actual housework. She could make simples and poultices, but not a meal or bread. She could treat minor wounds and illnesses, but not anything serious. She could sing and play the piano, but not well enough to be paid for it.

"I am a competent seamstress. Perhaps I could do that?" She did not sound enthusiastic. Lion had it on the tip of his tongue to point out that seamstresses were so poorly paid that many young attractive females supplemented their income from sewing by selling their bodies. Not an appropriate thing to say to a gently-born maiden, but he'd be damned if he let it come to that.

Blythe put what Lion had been thinking in more acceptable language. "Seamstresses don't make enough to live on, mostly. My sister manages because Ma don't charge except for her food. Maybe if you could work for a top dressmaker? They pay better, my sister says."

Miss Brabant wrinkled her nose. "I don't think I sew well enough or fast enough for that. Perhaps I could be a governess? I am sure I could teach other girls the skills that have been taught to me. But who would employ a governess who has run away from her father and the man her father chose for her?"

Who indeed? Lion didn't have an answer. Or, at least, the answer that was clamouring in his head with increasing fervour was not one he should suggest. Even if he'd wanted a wife, even if it wasn't madness to offer marriage to this chance-met stranger, he could not offer her what she deserved. He would be a terrible match for her.

He was, as his grandfather had frequently pointed out, an illegitimate half-breed. He was probably a decade older than her in years, and much older still in experience. He was going back to war as soon as he'd obeyed his grandfather's summons, and he wouldn't be in England at all if Wellington had not ordered it.

He would spend the rest of his life as a soldier, and that was no life for the sheltered daughter of a wealthy industrialist. He would have to think of something else, because he was not going to abandon her to the mercies of her father and her unwanted betrothed.

Miss Brabant changed the subject. "Where are you headed, Colonel O'Toole, if I might make so bold to ask?"

"Persham Abbey, in County Durham," the colonel answered. "I should be in Portugal with my men, but my grandfather summoned me home, and the general ordered me to obey." He shrugged. "Though why Wellington should care what Ruthford wants with me, I have no idea."

His next words were for himself. "Nor why Ruthford might want me. The old man never wanted the boy his son got without benefit of marriage. He got rid of me to school and then to the army soon enough."

He looked up to catch her watching. "My apologies for speaking in such a manner, Miss Brabant. I forgot myself for a moment." *Though perhaps it was as well for her to know how ineligible he was.*

"Not at all, Colonel. I take it your parents are no longer with us? I am sorry for your losses."

"I am not sure which Ruthford resents most," the colonel confided. "That my mother's mother was a Bengali woman, or that my mother's father was Irish and a common sergeant." He shrugged. "A most uncommon sergeant, to tell the truth."

He found himself telling her a story about his Grandfather O'Toole, an ox-cart, and a road that was nothing but mud for miles. She listened intently, laughing when he meant to be funny, gasping when the cover on the cart was thrown back to disclose the bandits, clapping at the victorious end.

One tale followed another. His boyhood in India, some of his and Fox's escapades in their schooldays, their service to the Crown in far-flung parts of the world. He occasionally called on Blythe for a word of corroboration, but Miss Brabant said little as the miles flew by on the wings of his stories.

They stopped at Northallerton for long enough to give the driver and groom a break and to have a meal themselves. Lion ordered a private room, once again claiming Dorothea as his sister. He requested washing water and whatever else she needed to refresh herself, and told her to fetch him when she was ready for lunch. While he waited, he ordered an ale at the public bar while he tried to think of a solution to the lady's problem.

Marriage was the best solution, but to whom? He had friends from school, but most of them held titles, and she had been clear about her distaste for the ton and all its denizens. He knew half a dozen officers who would offer for her in a heartbeat, but the army was no life for a woman. Besides, the thought of her with any of them revolted him. Not one of them was good enough for her.

Colonel O'Toole was such a nice man, and far less grim than he at first appeared. It was clear to Dorothea the corporal near worshipped him, and Dorothea had always thought that one could tell a lot about people by watching their servants. Roderick's servants loathed and feared him, and Roderick had frequently complained that they seldom stayed in his employ above a three-month.

As Dorothea washed and tidied herself, she reflected on the conversation in the carriage. She should be more disheartened than she was. She was no nearer to finding a way to stay free of her father and the loathsome Roderick than she had been when she first took refuge in the luggage box. She was hopeful, though, that the colonel would think of something. He was not obliged to concern himself with her problems, but he had done so, and she was certain he would not give up until she was safely settled.

Mrs Austin, the matron Father had paid to introduce her to Society, would say marriage was the only answer. Mrs Austin, however, saw nothing wrong with the betrothal to Roderick. "But you will be a countess," had been her only response to Dorothea's list of Roderick's faults. Every other suitor had been either unacceptable to her father or even worse than Roderick.

For a moment, Dorothea allowed herself to fantasise that she was married to Colonel O'Toole, that his kindness and consideration—and the gentle touch of his hands—would be hers for the asking. He was handsome, too—a man in the prime of his life. Thinking about his body, so muscular and strong, gave her a shiver, like a sudden fright, but not unpleasant. She splashed some more water on her suddenly hot cheeks.

He was not out of her reach, either. He had aristocratic relatives, but he was not himself of the upper classes. He was illegitimate, and a soldier. She was sorry for his sake about the way he had been treated by his grandfather and most of the earl's family. Dorothea knew, all too well, how it felt to be punished for the circumstances of her birth. She didn't care a whit for such things herself. He was everything she could desire in a man.

"Don't be foolish, Dorothea," she scolded herself. "What does a silly girl like you have to offer a man like him?" She knew nothing of his world. She knew nothing at all of much value. The scandal of her abduction and jilting would follow her into marriage. Father would cut her off for marrying to disoblige him. Marrying the colonel, even if he could be persuaded to consider it, would be a very poor return for his kindness.

She was ready, and she did not wish to keep the colonel waiting. She opened the door, and stepped out, straight into the path of Mrs Austin.

"Dorothea Brabant!" the lady shouted, at the top of her voice. "You dreadful girl! Do you know what you have done?"

Colonel O'Toole appeared at Mrs Austin's elbow. "Step this way, madam, and we shall discuss matters in private," he said, firmly.

At no less volume, Mrs Austin bellowed, "Is this the man you ran off with? A sight better looking than Westinghouse, I suppose, but your father…"

She broke off when Colonel O'Toole grabbed her by the elbow to walk her, whether she would or not, into the private room. Dorothea followed, closing the door behind them.

"Mrs Austin, I beg of you to be quiet," she said, as Mrs Austin shrieked her outrage. The woman ignored her.

Colonel O'Toole had had enough. "Silence, or I shall gag you," he said, glowering.

Even Dorothea felt a chill at the anger in his voice. Mrs Austin stopped mid shriek.

"Mrs Austin is the sponsor you mentioned to me?" the colonel asked Dorothea, in his usual pleasant tone, his anger gone as if it had never been.

Dorothea nodded. "She was. Father dismissed her when he decided to take me to York."

Colonel O'Toole regarded the now silent Mrs Austin with narrowed eyes. "I expect he did not want her to interfere with his plot to have you abducted and ruined," he said. "A respectable woman like Mrs Austin would not have wanted to be part of such an illegal action."

Dorothea thought that Mrs Austin would ignore anything she was paid not to see. The woman had not been much use as a sponsor, since she lacked the connections Dorothea needed to attend the better entertainments. Nor had she been a pleasant companion. Not unpleasant. Just bored by the activities Dorothea enjoyed, and excited all the things Dorothea disliked most about the Season— about fashion and gossip and status.

However, Mrs Austin was nodding vigorously in response to the colonel's remark. "I would not, indeed. The idea of it!" She narrowed her eyes at Dorothea, then turned on Colonel O'Toole. "Is that how it was? Her awful father paid you to abduct his daughter? Punishment, no doubt, for her defiant behaviour. He had arranged a marriage for her far higher than the likes of her could expect and she had refused, merely because the man was not to her taste."

Without moving, Colonel O'Toole somehow managed to loom larger, fixing Mrs Austin with furious eyes, so she cringed before him. "You impugn my honour, Mrs Austin, and Miss Brabant's" he said. "I rescued Miss Brabant from her abductor and am taking her to safety.

Mrs Austin looked around the room. "And yet I see no chaperone," she sneered. "Who is going to keep Miss Brabant safe from you? Or is it too late?"

Dorothea had had enough. "How dare you. The Colonel has been everything gentlemanly. You may say what you wish about me, though I have done nothing to deserve it, but to say he might do anything dishonourable, and for money, at that! It is disgusting, and I will not stand for it."

"That is as may be, Miss," Mrs Austin retorted, "but it is not what people will believe. You are ruined, and nobody will have you now. Unless it is this colonel of yours." She sneered again. "If he *is* a colonel."

The knock on the door came a moment before it opened. "Colonel, sir," said Corporal Blythe. "Oh. I beg your pardon, sir. I did not realise you had company."

"Mrs Austin is about to leave," Colonel O'Toole said, grimly. "Tell them to serve lunch, corporal. I want to be on the road again within the hour."

"Mrs Austin?" A lady intruded into the room; a matron in her middle years immaculately dressed in a travelling gown of beautifully embroidered wool. "So, this is where you got off to. I hope, Mrs Austin, you do not intend to wander off to have private conversations when you have charge of my daughter."

Mrs Austin curtseyed. "I beg your pardon, my lady. I was detained by these people."

"Lady Blaine," Colonel O'Toole said. "It is Lady Blaine, is it not?"

The lady lifted a lorgnette to examine him and raised both brows. "Surely you must be Lionel O'Toole? Lion, my dear boy! How charming to see you. But what are you doing in Northallerton?

No, do not tell me. Of course, you are going to Persham Abbey. Is the earl dying at last?"

"As far as I know, my lady, my grandfather is as fit as ever, and will outlive us all. But yes, I am bound for Persham Abbey."

She rapped the colonel's arm with her lorgnette. "Ruthford is very proud of you, Lion. Every time you are mentioned in despatches, we hear about it from him, and when you made colonel, one might have thought you had been appointed king. He won't tell you, of course. Too proud. So, I am letting you know myself."

Colonel O'Toole looked startled, but he said, "Then I thank you, my lady. May I ask after Anthony?"

"He is Lord Blaine now, and can you believe that his eldest daughter will be making her come-out in two years? Ridiculous how time passes. He will be delighted to hear I have seen you. I daresay he shall ride over to visit you while you are at the Abbey." She turned to Dorothea. "But I am being rude, my dear. You must forgive me. Lionel and my son Anthony were great friends in their school days."

Mrs Austin inserted herself. "This is Miss Brabant, my lady."

"My betrothed," the colonel added, taking Dorothea's hand and squeezing it in an unspoken message.

"The Brabant Mills heiress," Lady Blaine said. "Oh, well done, Lion. Congratulations. And my very best wishes to you, Miss Brabant. Lion is a splendid fellow. I am sure you will be very happy. But you are in a hurry. We will leave you to your lunch and hope to see you during your stay at the Abbey. Come along, Mrs Austin."

Dorothea protested as soon as the door shut behind the two women. "Betrothed?" Her heart had given a jump when he said it. He didn't mean it, of course. There was no use hoping he did, and the sooner she heard him say it was a ploy, the better.

"We'll discuss it in a minute," the colonel promised. "Corporal, give them the signal to serve lunch, would you?"

Dorothea sat drowning in her own contrary emotions as a couple of maids brought in trays, and laid everything out on the table. She had been drawn to the colonel from the first. *My instincts have been wrong in the past.* She trusted him. *I barely know him.*

If he really wanted to marry her, and was as wonderful as he seemed, that would solve all her problems. Her father would have no power over her. She would have a home, if only in a tent with the army. She would have a purpose. She would have Lionel O'Toole.

I will never again have to face the ton and their slurs and snubs. It would be almost worth it just for that.

If she married him, and he was not the man he appeared, she would lose everything. The freedom she had so briefly grasped, her chance of happiness. She had seen the misery of marriage to a tyrant.

The maids left, followed by Corporal Blythe.

Dorothea screwed up her courage. "You said 'betrothed'," she said.

Colonel O'Toole shrugged. "I know I should have asked properly before announcing it," he said, "but your former companion's intrusion, followed by that of Lady Blaine, rather forced the issue."

Dorothea did not know what to say. He had intended to ask her before Mrs Austin burst in?

He misunderstood her silence, because he rushed into speech. "If you do not like the idea, I will understand." It was the first time she had seen him discomposed. "I know I am much older than you, and I have already told you that I am not legitimate. My father was the eldest son of the Earl of Ruthford, but my mother was not even English."

Her own remembered rejections told her he was trying to discourage her, but she recognised the pain of old hurts in his eyes and they emboldened her to say, "I am a merchant's daughter, tainted with trade. One of my grandfathers was a farmer and the other a shopkeeper. My father started as a millworker, and is a coarse man, with no idea about the manners expected polite company, and no interest in learning them. I am not pretty—too short, too plump, and ordinary in every way. If I marry without my father's approval, I will not even have a dowry to make me attractive. I will be twenty-one in three months—which is old for an unmarried woman. You cannot possibly want to be burdened with me. No one else ever has."

His gaze heated. "I don't care about your ancestors or your dowry," he countered. "I have money enough to keep us both in comfort. You are *very* pretty, at least to me. I prefer brown hair and dark eyes, and a complexion with a little colour in it to the pale wraiths that are fashionable." His eyes dropped lower, to her breasts, and then he met her eyes again. "You are not plump, you are delightfully curved." He chuckled. "I will allow that you are short, Dorothea. May I call you Dorothea?"

He reached out a hand to her, and she accepted it, though his touch scrambled her wits and it took her a moment to order her thoughts enough to say, "I do not care about your ancestors, either," she admitted. "And you are just the right age."

She blushed, wondering if she should tell him that his birth was an advantage to her. "That you don't belong in the ton is an attraction to me. I don't either. We are neither fish nor fowl. Too educated to fit in the world into which we were born. Too low-born to fit into the world of the upper classes."

"And we do not want to," Lion said, with a shudder. "Not that they're all bad. I have one or two friends from school days, and a few I've met in the army, but you are right. For the most part, they keep their distance and that suits me just fine. If we don't fit anywhere else, perhaps we fit together. Is that what you are thinking?"

Dorothea nodded. "Did you really think of marriage before Lady Blaine came?"

"Yes. Almost from the first."

There was nothing but sincerity in every line of his face.

"I am no prize, Dorothea," he warned. "I was reluctant to ask. I hoped to find a solution that would not burden you with me."

"It would not be a burden, but a privilege," she protested.

"I am a military man, and must go back to war as soon as I have seen my grandfather."

"I would not mind living in a tent and travelling with the army. Not if I can be with you."

"Ah, Dorothea," he said, and he lifted her hand to place a kiss within the palm. "Is that a 'yes', then? You will marry me?"

"If you truly want me," she agreed.

He kissed her palm again. "Then eat your meal before it gets cold, my love. We have a long way to go and must be on our way soon."

CHAPTER 4

As Lion handed Dorothea down from the carriage in the village nearest to Persham Abbey, he was sorely tempted to ask the innkeeper for a room for the night. She looked tired, and no wonder. They had raced for Scotland, arriving in the middle of the afternoon of their third day out from Northallerton, had stayed one night after their perfunctory marriage over the anvil, and had hurried back to County Durham, to the delayed appointment with Lion's grandfather.

They could be at Persham Abbey with another twenty minutes travel. The Abbey on its bluff loomed above them, a ten-minute climb away, but the road meandered around the more gentle slopes on the other side.

First, though, he had promised Dorothea time to clean up and change, and to armour herself in one of the new gowns they had purchased in Carlisle. He understood her desire to look her best. He planned to wash and change into his dress uniform.

He smiled down at his wife. All that travelling, and she had not complained once. Nor had the nights in one inn after another been entirely devoted to sleep, at least on the return journey. Lion felt his lips curve upward at the memories. Dorothea might be small in stature, but her lush body was all female, and her passionate responses to his tutoring had him hardening again at the mere thought.

Indeed, after years of denying the urges of his body, he had only to turn to his wife, and his desires were met. Marrying Dorothea might be the best idea he had ever had.

"I've hired a room, Colonel," Blythe reported, "and ordered a bath." He blushed as he avoided Dorothea's eyes. The corporal had been relegated to the groom's perch behind the carriage for the last several days, and he must be aware of the use the newly-weds had made of their privacy for at least some of that time.

The rest of the time they had talked. She had told him about her lonely childhood with a dear but rather silly aunt and a succession of governesses. She had related some of her experiences during her London Seasons. "I think perhaps if I had submitted to the bullies they might have left me alone," she confided. "But I could not bear to do so. My father turns to threats and violence when anyone denies him, and I've never been able to stand up to him. But I was not going to let anyone else do it."

Lion had shared in return. His childhood in India, following the army of the East India Company, in which his father was an officer and his Irish grandfather a sergeant. His youth in England, spent mostly at school. His years ever since with the army; in Egypt, the Caribbean, Southern Africa, the East and, more recently, Spain and Portugal.

He even told her about Lady Diana, who had the features of a golden-haired angel and who had encouraged his courtship when he was a young officer of nineteen, and she the visiting daughter of a general. "It was just a game she was playing to amuse herself," he told Dorothea. "She told me so, when I proposed." Her words still cut, though he had long since recovered from his infatuation, and was even grateful for the lesson.

You are a commoner, base-born, landless and poor. I shall marry someone worthy of me, she had said. *You need to watch their eyes*, said his cousin Fox, when he returned from patrol to find Lion seething with rage and resentment. *Diana's eyes are cold as a snake's*. Dorothea's warm eyes showed her every emotion. He was fairly certain he had never smiled as much in his life as he had in the past few days.

Dorothea was particularly interested in his current command, for she had insisted that she wanted to return to Portugal with him, and Lion was torn. On the one hand, he could not help but neglect her while he attended to his command. On the other, she had quickly become as essential to him as breathing, and he did not want to be parted from her.

The landlady showed them upstairs, her eyes gleaming with interest. This close to the Abbey, everyone knew the earl's bastard grandson who had gone for a soldier. She was clearly in a fever of curiosity about Lion's sudden marriage. Lion thanked her politely, and ushered her away as soon as the bath was in place.

With a huge effort of will, Lion managed not to be distracted as they bathed and dressed again, though he did have to help Dorothea with her laces and her buttons. She sat before the looking glass to do her hair. "Take your time, my love," he said. "I'll get a message away to the Abbey letting them know we will be there within the hour. No need to rush. Come down when you are ready."

He went downstairs to the entry hall, and asked the manager for pen and paper, then sat to write his note. He was folding it and sealing it when a familiar voice said his name. "Lion! You're here!"

Lion was pleased to see his cousin. "Fox. You did reach the Abbey before me after all. Or are you on the way there now?"

"I arrived two days ago, expecting you to be days before me. Imagine my surprise, colonel, when I was informed that Lion the monk had been distracted by a skirt. I see you have managed to ditch the chit. You'll have to tell her father and her suitor where they can find her. They are cluttering up the Abbey, at the moment, and annoying grandfather, who, by the way, is refusing to say why we were summoned until you arrive."

Fox's wry look invited Lion to laugh with him. "Apparently, he is the only person permitted to find fault with you." He looked over Lion's shoulder. His eyes widened and his jaw dropped.

Dorothea was descending the stairs, and Lion didn't blame Fox for nearly swallowing his tongue. He'd seen the dinner gown on her before he came downstairs. It looked even better from a distance under the stair lamps, with her hair done up in curls, held in place by the jewelled pins he'd purchased in Carlisle, the matching parure adorning her neck, her ears, and her wrist.

He held out his hand, and she walked straight to him, ignoring the men who stood gaping—guests and staff alike. Lion bowed over her hand and kissed it. "My love, allow me to make known to you my cousin, Major James Foxton. His mother was my father's sister, so we share a grandfather. Fox, Dorothea has done me the great honour of becoming my wife. I hope the pair of you will become friends."

Fox was ready with a charming bow and a smile. "Mrs O'Toole, I am delighted to meet you."

Dorothea dipped a curtsey. "And I you, Major Foxton. I have been looking forward to meeting my husband's dear friend. His first friend in England, he said, and the man who has saved his life on several occasions."

Fox chuckled. "The honours are about even, I think, Mrs O'Toole. He has also saved mine. By the way, I have already had the pleasure of meeting your betrothed and your father." Springing it on Dorothea like that was Fox's idea of a joke. Lion would have to have a word with him, in private, about not honing his wit on Lion's wife.

Dorothea cast a startled glance around the room. "They are here?"

"At the Abbey, dear heart," Lion said. "Fox came down to warn us."

Fox laughed. "I can make no claim to be such a Samaritan. I had no idea you would be here, but came down to get away from the dreadful atmosphere. The earl is in his room sulking, and our uninvited guests are in the main parlour running Lion's character down. It was entirely fortuitous that the first person I saw here when I walked in the door was Lion. You are in for a scolding, I fear, Mrs O'Toole."

Dorothea lifted her chin in a gesture of defiant pride. "Only my husband has the right to scold me, Major Foxton, but my father will certainly make the attempt. As for Mr Westinghouse, I never accepted his proposal and owe him nothing. However, I thank you for the warning."

Fox raised his eyebrows, and his smile was all admiration. "Lion, my friend, I quite see why you married the lady."

He hitched his horse behind their carriage and rode with them, doing his best to exercise his charm on Dorothea. However, she was clearly nervous about the coming interviews, because she sat quietly, responding briefly and politely to his sallies, but without the flirtatious conversation Fox obviously expected. Her hand in Lion's was tense.

He wished Fox had not come with them, so he could hold her in his arms and give her comfort. "No need to accompany us, Fox," he had said. "Stay and have the drink you came for."

Fox, though, said he never could resist a fireworks show.

By the time the carriage arrived at Persham Abbey, Lion had a plan. "Fox, go on in and distract Brabant and Westinghouse, will you? Dorothea, we will slip in the side door. Best we go and visit the earl before we deal with your father, do you not think?"

Fox laughed. "His willingness to sacrifice the troops to win the ramparts is what made him a colonel, Mrs O'Toole." He dashed off a mocking salute. "I'll protect your flank, cousin, while you make a sneak assault on the throne room. But you will let me watch when you meet with Westinghouse, will you not?"

As he walked away, Lion gave Dorothea's hand a gentle squeeze. Did Fox have to treat everything as a joke? He had upset Dorothea with his nonsense. "Everything will be fine," Lion promised her. "None of them have any power over us, my wife."

Her smile was a little shaky, but her return squeeze was firm. "Then let us go and meet your grandfather, Lionel."

The Earl of Ruthford had pale blue eyes under fearsomely bushy eyebrows. The eyes fixed on Dorothea when she and

Lion were permitted into the earl's private sitting room, and the brows drew together in a glare, but his words were for Lionel. "So, you deign to come to see me at last." He did not stand. Was he making it clear that Dorothea was not a lady?

"I came as soon as my obligations permitted, my lord," Lion had noticed the rudeness, and was scowling.

"Your obligations? Your pleasures, more like. Is this the chit you ran off with?" the earl asked, rudely, glaring even more fiercely.

Lion was not intimidated. "Grandfather, the lady is my wife, Dorothea. Dorothea, this rude gentleman is my grandfather, the Earl of Ruthford."

The earl ignored Lion and addressed Dorothea. "So, you are the Brabant girl," he said. "Your father, young lady, is a bombastic old fool."

"It would be unfilial of me to agree and impolite to disagree, my lord," Dorothea told him, catching the wince as he shifted to be comfortable. Perhaps he did not stand because he could not. He was, after all, a very old man.

The earl made a harrumphing noise then changed targets again. "A sudden marriage, Lion. You could not have got the girl with child, or, at least, you could not know whether you have. You arrived in England ten days ago, and cannot have known your wife above a sennight."

He turned his cold eyes on Dorothea again. "Are you breeding, girl?"

Dorothea was tired of bullies, and she did not need to fear this one. Lionel would protect her. Still, he had a family right to be curious, if not to be rude. "My name is Dorothea, my lord. Not chit and not girl. If I am enceinte, it is too early to know. I have been married barely four days, and I went a maid to my marriage bed."

To her surprise, the earl chuckled and relaxed back against his pillows. "Lady Blaine said you were not a milk and water miss. After I met your father-in-law, Lionel, I had my doubts about the marriage, but Lady Blaine assured me the girl was raised as a lady and is up to your weight. I begin to think she may be right. Well, here we are. Sit down the pair of you. You must forgive me,

Dorothea, for not standing when you entered. I need a footman to get me out of my chair these days. Cursed old age."

Lion took a seat beside Dorothea on a sofa, and took her hand. She studied his face, which he had composed into a blank mask again, but she knew him well enough now to see his grandfather's revelation had worried him. For all his resentment of the man, he still cared about him. She squeezed his hand in sympathy.

The earl was still talking. "Tell me how you came to meet, my children. I can guess why you had to marry. I have met that nasty piece of work, Westinghouse. You'll have to deal with him, Lionel. He will damage our Dorothea's reputation if he can."

Dorothea had gone from this chit, to the girl, to our Dorothea in the space of a few minutes. She felt dazed.

"I will handle them both," Lionel promised.

"I have no doubt of it," said the earl. "Now. How much of the tarradiddle I was told was true? Clearly you did not seduce and abandon her. Did you elope with her from York? How was Westinghouse involved? For I'm sure if any nasty behaviour occurred, he was the villain."

Dorothea noticed, if Lion didn't, the earl's confidence that Lion's behaviour had been exemplary, and warmed to the old man still further.

They spent nearly three quarters of an hour in quiet chat with the earl, until his valet interrupted. "Forgive me, my lord, but it is time for your medicine."

The earl sighed. "I must take my rest, my dear," he said to Dorothea, "Or I shall not be fit to attend dinner, and I would not miss it for the world. Lion, my boy, we have not spoken of the reason I sent for you. I promise to reveal all at dinner, but for now I must obey my physician."

Lion nodded and Dorothea, on an impulse, kissed the earl on his cheek. He froze in shock, and then his craggy face softened into a warm smile. "You are a dear girl, Dorothea. I am glad Lionel found you."

"Good lord," said Lion, as he escorted Dorothea along the passage from the earl's rooms. "I have never seen my grandfather so… so amiable. He must be really sick. I had no idea. I wonder why Fox did not mention it?"

Dorothea was just relieved that the interview was over, though it had been much more pleasant than she expected. "Do you think that is why he summoned you, Lionel? Because he was sick?"

Lion grimaced, a contortion that involved shrugged eyebrows and a twisted mouth. *I don't know,* the expression said. "Shall I find out where our room is?" he asked, changing the subject. "Let me see your father while you rest, and perhaps smooth things over before you have to meet him. Or turn him out if he is likely to be rude to you."

"I will see him with you, Lionel," Dorothea insisted. "He *is* going to be rude, but I am used to that. I want him to know he cannot bully me any more." She could not resist a chuckle at the thought of her father's reaction. "He is going to be surprised."

A footman directed them to the billiards room. "Mr Brabant is there with Major Foxton and Mr Westinghouse, sir," he told Lion.

Dorothea quailed a little at the idea of facing Roderick, as well as her father, but she did her best to hide her reaction from Lion. She was determined to show her husband she could be a courageous army wife, able to hold her own in what he had described as the rough life of dragoons on campaign.

He caught her trepidation, though, and stopped, looking down at her with one eyebrow raised in question.

"Let's get it done, my husband," she said.

"Let's get it done," he agreed.

Only Major Foxton noticed their arrival. He was standing back from the table, leaning on his cue, watching the other two men with the faint amusement that seemed to characterise him. Dorothea was determined to like the major for her husband's sake, but so far, he seemed to be a typical sneering aristocrat, albeit with a veneer of charm over his scorn.

Father was taking his shot, and Roderick was leaning over to watch so closely that Father must feel the oaf's breath on his cheek. Dorothea, in a spurt of malice, hoped that breath stunk as much as when Roderick had forced kisses on her.

Lion led Dorothea around the table, to Major Foxton. "Stay here with Fox," he murmured. "Let me speak first."

He expressed it as a command, though his eyes made it a request. She supposed he was in the habit of giving orders. He was going to have to learn that Dorothea was not one of his soldiers, but this was not the moment. She nodded.

Lion moved several paces away along the room and waited for Brabant to make his shot, which he did, after snarling at Roderick to give him space. He failed to sink his ball, and shook his cue at Roderick as he straightened. "Damn you, Westinghouse. You put me off."

"Mr Brabant," Lion said. "I believe you have been expecting me."

Father and Roderick both turned their attention to Lion.

"You are the blackamore bastard who ruined my daughter," Father snarled.

Lion snapped his heels together and made a shallow bow. "I am Colonel Lionel O'Toole of the 25th Dragoons, sir, and also have the honour of being husband to the former Dorothea Brabant, now Mrs O'Toole."

"A damned blackamoor and Irish!" Roderick growled, his words slurred with drink.

"You will not curse in front of my wife," Lion told him. "You are, I take it, the villain who abducted my wife? It would be my great pleasure, Westinghouse, to knock out a couple of your teeth, so please give me an excuse."

Father puffed out his chest and jutted his chin. "I sent my daughter with Mr Westinghouse so he could gain her consent to the marriage I had approved," he said. "I will have your marriage annulled, for it was in breach of the promise to Mr Westinghouse."

Lion regarded him with thinly veiled contempt. "You sent your daughter to be ravished by a violent drunkard, and bullied into a marriage that would have been a living hell. If you wish to air your scandalous behaviour by going through the courts, Mr Brabant, go ahead. You will lose. Mrs O'Toole made no promises to Mr Westinghouse, and it is only her wits and her courage that brought her safely away."

"Damn bitch hit me on the head," Roderick complained.

Lion took a step towards him and laid him out with one punch, then grabbed him by the collar and pulled him up, his fist back to hit him again. Dorothea started forward and laid a hand on his arm. "Lionel, he is out cold," she said.

Lion turned burning eyes upon her, his face a mask of rage, but then sense came back into his eyes. He dropped Roderick and laid a comforting hand over Dorothea's, before striding past Father to stare at the rack of billiard cues.

Father, Dorothea was intrigued to see, shrank as Lionel passed, curving his spine and tucking his chin into his chest as if in an effort to hide. As soon as he took his attention off Lionel, however, he saw Dorothea, and his indignation overcame his fear of her husband.

"Dorothea," he roared. "Come here, you deceitful disobedient hellion."

Dorothea stayed where she was, and Lion was quick to step between her and her father. He had himself under full control again. "My wife does not answer to you, Mr Brabant," he warned.

"Let her tell me that in her own words," Brabant demanded. "She has always been a good, obedient girl. What have you done with her, O'Toole? Have you bewitched her with some sort of foreign hocus pocus?"

Dorothea refused to let that stand. She stepped up beside Lionel. "My husband won me with his respect and his integrity, Father. When I fled from the villain to whom you wanted me tied, he listened to me and he helped me. He does not treat me as a pawn to be pushed around the board for your benefit, but as an intelligent human being; a partner to be trusted. I have given him myself in marriage. I owe him my obedience. Now and for all of our lives, he will always come first for me. I no longer answer to you."

"But Dorothea," Father protested. "You could have been a countess."

CHAPTER 5

R oderick did not come down to dinner, Father was sulking, and the earl was obviously tired and in pain, but snapped at anyone who dared to express concern. Lionel introduced Dorothea to the hostess, the earl's unmarried sister, Lady Patricia Strathford-Bowles, who was welcoming. The distracted and anxious glances the lady kept shooting at her brother might have had nothing to do with Dorothea.

Lionel had timed their descent so he did not have to put her through the ordeal of introductions to the mixed crowd of dependents, hangers on, and neighbours. Lion had explained that the earl seldom sat down to dinner with fewer than twenty settings, and considered it his bounden duty to offer hospitality to anyone of appropriate birth who asked for it. "If anyone insults you, Dorothea," he had said, "apply to me."

Lion's friend Lord Blaine and his wife—the only people she would have liked to meet—were not in attendance. The Dowager Lady Blaine stopped them on their way into dinner to confide that the couple had another engagement, but that her son would be over to see Lion as soon as possible.

Dorothea was pleased to find herself seated between Lionel and the earl, and thus spared the need to converse with the large group of strangers, most of whom stared at her with avid eyes, and some with hostility.

The meal itself was pleasanter than expected. Major Foxton and Lady Blaine were determined to be cheerful and entertaining, and others followed their lead.

The shock came after dinner was over. Lady Patricia stood as a signal to the ladies that it was time to leave the room.

The earl shook his head and she resumed her seat. The earl tapped a spoon on his glass to demand silence. He let his gaze travel around the table, finishing with Lionel and Dorothea. "I have given much thought to what I wanted to say, and how to say it," he began.

"I have chosen this occasion because my grandson deserves that the news I am about to share is spread as far as possible, and I shall count on those here at my table to pass on the story I am about to relate."

The corner of his mouth quirked in a fraction of a smile. "Lionel, here, is going to ask why I did not warn him. Well, all I can say in my defence is that, when I planned this dinner party, I expected him to have been here well before it. Lion, I hope you will agree that today, your news took priority over mine."

Lion inclined his head.

The earl stared into his glass as if for inspiration, then straightened his shoulders and lifted his chin. "Nineteen years ago, my grandson arrived from India, with documents that proved he was the son of my deceased eldest son, Anthony Lord Harcourt. According to the papers the boy bought with him, his mother was the daughter of an Indian woman and an Irish sergeant, and he had been living with the sergeant since his mother died."

He closed his eyes for a moment, and his knuckles were white as he gripped the table. "One of the documents claimed to be a copy of a marriage record between my son and the boy's mother, I did not believe it. My son had never written of a marriage. Indeed, he had never mentioned the woman at all, though he had told his Aunt Patricia about his son. The boy had been told he bore Harcourt's surname, as did his mother, but it was easier for me to believe that he had been lied to than that Harcourt had hidden such a mesalliance from me."

Beside Dorothea, Lionel sat frozen in place, and when Dorothea put her hand on his to assure him of her support, the skin beneath her fingers felt cold to the touch.

The earl took another deep breath and looked around the table, his eyes not pausing until they met Lion's. After a long moment, he lowered his head and continued his story. "My second son had been recognised as Viscount Harcourt since word came of his brother's death five years earlier. I did not bother him with the contents of the package of documents. Indeed, no one knew what it contained except myself. Not even Lionel. The courier who brought him gave it to me with the seal unbroken. Nonetheless, I sent agents to discover the facts."

The hand under Dorothea's tensed further, which should not have been possible.

Another deep breath, this one released in a shuddering sigh. "All the adults in the story were dead. My son. Sergeant O'Toole. O'Toole's daughter and his wife. It took time for my agents to uncover witnesses who could speak to the truth. By the time the agents returned, two years had passed. My second son had been known everywhere as Lord Harcourt for seven years. Seven years! Lion had been accepted as my illegitimate but recognised grandson."

With a sigh, his hands shaking, he faced Lion. His eyes were anguished as he said. "Lionel, I will not ask for your forgiveness, for I do not deserve it. My agents found witnesses to your parents' marriage, including the wife of the parson who performed the service. The parson had also died, but his wife was at the wedding and swore it was a true and legal union."

The earl, his voice strained but still firm, continued, "But to tell Harry he was not the heir; to tell his wife! You were already speaking of a military career. I decided to say nothing; to leave matters as they were. It was a dreadful thing to do. I knew it at the time. I knew it every time I looked at you from the day I knew I had wronged you."

Lion's face had turned as hard as granite and his voice was husky as if forced through an unmoving throat. "My parents were truly married?"

The earl nodded. "You are the legitimate son of my eldest son and my heir. When your uncle and his son died, I notified the Committee for Privileges. They have confirmed you as Viscount Harcourt, and you will be Earl of Ruthford after me, which will be soon."

Lionel said nothing, but he gripped Dorothea's hand hard enough for her to hide a wince.

Major Foxton leapt to his feet and hurried around the table, sporting a broad smile. "Lion, that is wonderful. Grandfather, you must be delighted. I know how proud you are of my cousin. Lion will be a superlative earl. As one of those under his command, I can assure you of that." He reached Lionel and gave his shoulder a robust punch. "We must have champagne! I cannot think of anyone who deserves a peerage more! Just think how thrilled the tenants and servants will be not to be subjected to our second cousin and his wife!"

Following Major Foxton's lead, the others at the table stood to offer their own congratulations. Lionel stood to receive them, baring his teeth in a parody of a smile, clinging to Dorothea's hand as if he feared being swept under by the surge of goodwill.

"I don't want it," he hissed out of the corner of his mouth. But Major Foxton and the earl both pretended they had not heard, and nobody else was listening.

Footmen began moving through the crowd with trays of champagne, but the earl sent them to the drawing room. The guests and family followed along, a footman pushing the earl in his chair. Somehow, Dorothea became separated from Lionel, and found herself faced by a wall of backs as she attempted to return to his side.

Her father grabbed her arm before she tried to penetrate the obstacle. "Well done, puss," he said. "You will be a countess, just as I planned! And no risk that Westinghouse's brother's wife might die, allowing him to marry again and have sons! I could not be more proud. How did you know?"

"I did not know, Father," Dorothea insisted, suppressing a sigh as she realised Roderick had joined the after-dinner celebrations.

"You lie, you bitch," Roderick grumbled. He loomed over to the two of them, snarling. "As for you, Brabant, you promised me a bride. You owe me, and I mean to collect."

Lion's deep voice spoke as his arm slipped supportively around Dorothea's back. "That is between you and Mr Brabant, Westing-house. As for me and my wife, I am exercising the privilege of newly-weds, and we are saying good night." He raised his voice. "Good evening to you all. Thank you for your good wishes."

"I shall say good night, too," the earl announced. "Lionel, would you be good enough to push my chair to the stairs? Thank you to you all for coming this evening, and for your support for my grandson. Please continue to enjoy yourselves. Dorothea, come along, my dear."

Their lovemaking that night had an edge of feverish desperation, but by morning Lion had woken in a more philo-sophical frame of mind. "Perhaps the earl did me a favour," he said, when she asked him how he was. She had woken in his arms, as she had every night since Gretna Green.

"How so?" she asked.

"He would never have let me go into the army had I been named his heir when I was a boy." His smile was grim. "Or he would have asked for me to be given the most dangerous assign-ments so I was removed from the way of those with purer blood. Either way, the career I have had is my own."

He rolled her, then, so she lay flat on the bed with him above her, his legs stretched between hers, his weight held on his elbows. "But I have cheated you, Dorothea. You thought yourself safe from marriage to a nobleman, and now look!"

"You are still my Lionel, and I am your Dorothea," she reminded him. "For your sake, I will make the best of it." She had puzzled it out for herself last night, while Lion was pacing the room, despairing over the loss of his military career. Indeed, he had lost more than her, since the earl's heir she had inadvertently married was the man she wanted to be with for the rest of her life, whereas he would have to leave the army when his grandfather died.

Not before, he had insisted last night.

"But won't the earl want us to stay now that he has named you his heir?" she had said.

The corners of his mouth had quirked in a wicked smile. "He has no say in where I go and what I do. I do not need his money, and nor does he have influence that will remove me from my post."

So they were still bound for Portugal, and Dorothea was glad of it; glad of a year or two to become accustomed to marriage before they had to face the duties neither of them wanted.

Lion kissed her nose. "Are you tired of travelling? Would you like a few days rest before we leave for Portugal?"

"You are anxious to get back," Dorothea said.

He kissed her again, a soft brush of his lips to the top of her head. "I am asking what you want," he pointed out.

Whatever you want. But he would not accept that answer. "I would be delighted to leave Father behind, and to start our real life together."

"Good," said Lion. "Enough talking. All I want from you in the next half hour, wife of mine, are moans, the word more, and perhaps my name."

And he made it so.

After breakfast in their room and a bath, they went down to announce their intentions.

The earl was surprisingly philosophical. "I did not expect you to give up your command in the middle of a campaign, Lionel," he said. "Just be careful, boy. Young James is not wrong about my great nephew and his wife. They would be a disaster for the estates." He shrugged. "But I lost any right to tell you what to do when I lied to you."

He frowned in thought. "Would it not make sense, though, to send messages to find out what ships are heading to Portugal and when, and wait here in comfort until your passage is arranged?"

Lion nodded slowly. "That does make sense," he said. "Would you mind, Dorothea?"

Dorothea was disappointed, but she agreed. They would be on their way soon enough, after all. Indeed, Lion wasted no time. He led her to the library, where he wrote several letters and entrusted them to grooms to take to the mail.

Father, when they told him, was preparing to leave Persham Abbey. He had business meetings to attend, he explained, and now his daughter was settled, he was leaving for York this morning.

He was horrified to hear Lion was planning to allow Dorothea to go with him. "Lord Harcourt!" It took Dorothea a moment to realise he meant Lion. Of course, her husband was now Lord Harcourt. How very strange. Father was still protesting. "No! I cannot permit it. My daughter was not raised to follow the drum! No, indeed. Dorothea, you cannot go."

Lionel smiled at her. "My wife will answer you, Mr Brabant. I am determined not to be a domestic tyrant."

Dorothea's heart swelled with love. He said nothing of the arguments they had already had about her determination to remain with him. Instead, he gave her his unqualified support, and also his trust.

"Father," she said, firmly. "You raised me to know my duty, and I have tried to do it. Now, my duty is no longer to my father but to my husband. I cannot do that duty in England when he is in Portugal."

Father frowned. "Ah. You mean giving him an heir. Yes. I can see that is of the utmost importance."

No. That was not what she meant. But if it would keep Father from making a fuss, she would let him believe that was her purpose.

Father was addressing Lionel. "You will keep her safe?"

"She will not be in danger," Lionel assured him. Dorothea had argued with him most of the way from Scotland, and his main concern was he did not want to put her in danger, but she would let him console her father, even if the man did not deserve it.

They had the consent, if not the approval, of the heads of both of their families, even if they did not need it. The most surprising and vociferous objection came from Lionel's cousin, James Foxton.

"Lion, what are you thinking? You are Harcourt, now. Heir to all of this. Your place is here, beside our grandfather. Surely you will be leaving the army to do your duty here?"

"My place is with my men," Lion said, firmly.

"Our men," Major Foxton commented. "You won't be letting the men down, Lion. Recommend me for the command, and Bear Gavenor for a promotion. I can lead them, with Cassiday and Gavenor as my majors."

Lion's sigh hinted this was not a new argument. "Fox, the four of us are a formidable team: Bear with the exploring officers, you and Michael in charge of a squadron each, and me co-ordinating the whole. Let's face it. We are all needed. After the Russian disaster, the French are short of men in Spain, and strung out across a country-wide front. Wellington will advance soon, and he will need us at our best. I'm going back. The job isn't done until we've driven the French out of Spain."

He smiled. "And you know how I hate to leave a job undone."

Major Foxton returned his smile with a jaunty grin of his own. "I can tell your mind is made up. And are you determined to drag your wife with you?"

Dorothea could speak for herself. "I am determined to go with my husband," she insisted.

The major shrugged. "There is nothing more to be said then. I'll have someone pack my things."

"We are not leaving yet, Fox," Lion told him. "You can relax for a few more days. Beat that swine Westinghouse at billiards a few more times. I've written to find out about passage."

Major Foxton nodded. "Good idea, if Lady Harcourt is to go with us." He smiled at Dorothea, but the smile did not reach his eyes. "We slung hammocks in the wardroom on the Pepper, but that will hardly do for a lady."

"I'll enjoy the comfort of a cabin myself," Lion commented.

"I'll bet," the major muttered, with a glance at Dorothea.

CHAPTER 6

As it happened, Major Foxton had no more opportunity to play billiards with Roderick, even though Roderick had not left with Father, as Dorothea had half expected.

He left later that day, though, and not willingly. Major Foxton and Roderick had apparently been playing for ever greater amounts of money, and Major Foxton had decided it was time for Roderick to pay up.

Dorothea didn't see the discussion, but several footmen did, and word soon spread through the house, reaching Dorothea through the maid who had been loaned to her for her stay.

"First, Mr Westinghouse tried to convince Major Foxton to give him a chance to win the money back, but Major Foxton said that Mr Westinghouse had a snowball's chance in he— in the bad place, my lady, because he was spectacularly bad at billiards."

Dorothea knew she should tell the maid not to gossip, but she was enjoying the story too much to stop it.

"I do not suppose Mr Westinghouse liked that," she said.

"Not at all," the maid agreed. "He said some hard things about Major Foxton, but Major Foxton just declared he was not just bad at billiards, but he was a bad loser. And not a gentleman, besides, if he could not pay his wagers." She paused the story while she judiciously placed a couple of hair pins with little enamelled flowers to adorn Dorothea's hair. She stepped back to examine the effect in the mirror and then added another.

"What did Mr Westinghouse say to that?" Dorothea asked, more interested in the story than her reflection, though she did admire the pretty pins, which Lion had purchased for her in the village.

"He said he did not have the money on him, but would forward it when he got back to York. Major Foxton said no. He said he was going back to Portugal and would have the money in cash, kind, or slices of Mr Westinghouse's flesh! Did you ever hear the like?"

A Shakespearean reference to Shylock's pound of flesh was clearly lost on the maid. Dorothea rather doubted Roderick understood it, either.

"Mr Westinghouse got into a rage and told Major Foxton that he was no gentleman if he did not trust Mr Westinghouse's word. Major Foxton said he knew precisely what value to place on the word of an abductor and rapist. Mr Westinghouse said some other hard things, and looked fit to murder, the footmen said. But Major Foxton is taller and stronger and fitter, and a soldier besides. Mr Westinghouse didn't dare. He went off in a rage, and Major Foxton let him go."

Dorothea heard the end of the affair at dinner. Major Foxton made an amusing story of it. Apparently, he had escorted Roderick and his luggage down to the village. The general merchant, who sometimes acted as a pawnbroker, accepted a cigarette case, three watch fobs, a snuff box, and a set of silver cuff buttons in return for sufficient money to satisfy Major Foxton.

"There was enough left over for a ticket on a stage coach back to York from the nearest market town," Major Foxton said. "I paid the innkeeper to send him there in the inn's chaise, and before he left, I bought him a meal to fortify him for the journey. We parted the best of friends, though that could have been because Westinghouse was half soused. My contribution to your honeymoon, Lion." His eyes twinkled and Lion laughed.

W ith Brabant and Westinghouse gone, Lion and Dorothea enjoyed a few glorious days of honeymoon while waiting for the results of Lion's letters.

He had written to the Admiralty and to each of the nearest naval stations enquiring about which of their ships were sailing for Portugal, preferably Porto. To cover his bets, he had also written to the nearest commercial ports asking about merchant ships that took passengers. These letters went to the harbourmasters in Newcastle, Edinburgh, Great Yarmouth, and Liverpool.

Meanwhile, they spent most of each day and all night together, every day. The earl said they should not bother with company unless they wished. They went for a visit to the Blaines, who were very welcoming to Lion's wife, though Dorothea commented to Lion afterwards that she found it disconcerting to be only a handful of years older than the daughter of one of Lion's closest friends.

Apart from that visit they seldom spent time with others in the household or the neighbourhood, instead eating in their room or taking a hamper out with them on long rambles around the estate and the neighbouring countryside. Rides, too, after Lion had given Dorothea a couple of lessons. She had never ridden before, but was determined to master the art, for Lion's stories made it clear that she would otherwise be relegated to a cart in the rear of the army.

Fox kept trying to get Lion off on some male-exclusive activity, or at least to persuade Lion to invite Fox to join him and Dorothea. Lion wasn't interested. "The time I can devote to Dorothea will be short enough," he pointed out after several such attempts. "If you're bored, Fox, go and visit friends. I'll let you know when we have to leave."

"Your problem," Fox grumbled, "is that you have been such a puritan that your humours were out of balance. A few days of good bed sport, and you are walking around in a happy glow that you mistake for being in love. You hardly know the woman."

"Be careful, Fox," Lion warned. "I will not tolerate insults to my wife." He left his cousin to his sulk.

He and Dorothea spent some time each day with the earl, however. Dorothea had suggested it. "He wronged you when he did not acknowledge you, Lion," she said. "And then he wronged you again when he allowed his guilt to push you away and treated you with coldness." She smiled and stroked his bristly cheek with her soft hand.

"I know you think he wronged you a third time when he at last told the truth, and made you heir to his earldom and all his responsibilities. He cannot understand that, Lion. He thinks he has made things right."

"You make things right," he said, placing a kiss in the palm that caressed him.

"He is dying, Lion. If you do not wish to make peace with him before he goes, then I support you. But this may be your only opportunity. Besides, he may have things to tell you that will help when you come to inherit the title and the estates."

He had not thought of that last point, but she was right. The idea of being earl was overwhelming, and it would be stupid to refuse any wisdom the man had to impart just because his feelings were hurt.

As it turned out, she had been right about making peace with the old man, too. They spent an hour with him twice a day, listening to his stories of the past and learning about the various estates and the people who worked for them. Lion still thought his grandfather a bigoted old autocrat, but he also recognised the other side of the man—a leader who loved the people and the land for which he was responsible. He may have been a neglectful husband, an indifferent father, and a tyrannical grandfather. But he was an excellent earl.

Lion's best times, though, were with Dorothea.

With her, Lion found a completeness he had never known. He enjoyed everything they did together. Walking, talking, playing cards, telling stories. Even just sitting quietly, absorbed in a book or paperwork or other work, and occasionally glancing up to meet eyes, smile, and return to their tasks.

For the first time since he was a cornet, just beginning his army career, he began to envisage making a life in peacetime. If only the earl had not dumped a title on him.

Best of all were those moments when passion was, for the moment, sated, and they lay in one another's arms. In those moments, before his desire rose again and hers ignited to meet him, he was at peace.

It lasted four nights. On the fourth day, Lion received a response from the Newcastle harbourmaster, with details of three ships that might meet their needs. He'd also heard about several naval ships, none of them large enough to have accommodation suitable for his wife. One of the commercial ships it would be, then.

He set the letters aside to deal with later. There was no hurry, since none of the appropriate ships sailed for another two weeks, and today he and Dorothea were riding up to a folly where there was a spectacular view over the estate, a lockable door, and a comfortable day bed.

He'd sent up a basket of food, sheets, and blankets, and they spent a long leisurely afternoon uncovering the view that gave him the most delight, and inspecting it closely, to the great pleasure of them both.

The following morning brought another message.

He opened it at the little table in their sitting room while Dorothea was still in the dressing room with her temporary maid. His oath brought her to the doorway, still in her underthings.

"Is something the matter, Lion?"

"General Picton is back in Portugal, and demands my presence," Lion said. "I don't want to leave you, my love, but I am going to have to take a berth on one of the navy's little sloops, and leave you to follow on the *Bellflower*." The *Bellflower* was the ship they had selected together the evening before.

She swallowed. "May I not come with you?"

"Not on a sloop, Dorothea, where we all sleep in the one room and the only privacy is a curtain hung from the ceiling. But you can come with me to Newcastle to book your passage and see me off."

She didn't argue, bless her dear soul. "I would like that. If I must be left behind, I should like our time apart to be as short as possible."

He wrote a message to the captain of the *Augusta*, seeking a berth to Porto in three days time, when the ship was expected in Newcastle. "We should be early, my love, in case the Augusta arrives early, for they won't delay for passengers."

"Today?" she asked, but Lion thought the next day would be good enough, and wrote another message to book rooms for him and his party at the Queen's Head.

Blythe, when told of their travel plans and given the messages to take to the stables, hesitated.

"Out with it, corporal," Lion said, recognising the expression of a soldier who thinks he should warn his commander of a possible mistake, but is afraid of the officer's reaction.

Blythe stood at attention, but his eyes shifted to Dorothea. "My lady's kit, sir," he said. "She might need to write ahead. Two weeks is not much time for a dressmaker."

Of course! "You are right, Blythe. Thank you."

Dorothea's face showed that she had no idea what they were talking about. "I have new clothes," she pointed out. "Plus, Father said he will send what I left in York.

"Darling," Lion said, "you need clothing enough for all four seasons, several pairs of stout shoes, soap and the like. Anything you might want while we are on the march and might not be able to buy in Portugal or Spain."

Dorothea's frown turned thoughtful. "Your great aunt may have some suggestions. Or Lady Blaine. But neither of them will be up at this time."

"Blythe," Lion said, "ask Lady Patricia's dresser whether her ladyship has any recommendations for modistes in Newcastle. Tell her Lady Harcourt requires a complete wardrobe suitable for summer campaigning in Spain. She will be awake, Dorothea. She takes her breakfast on a tray and steadfastly refuses to appear before midday. But I'm sure she is awake."

He proved to be correct. Within fifteen minutes, a footman

delivered a note from Lady Patricia with four names: one for practical day wear, one for sturdy foot wear, one for riding habits, and one for evening wear.

"You might find better modistes in London, Harcourt," the lady had written, "but these will do a commendable job, and quickly. Make appointments with them all, and tell them their deadline in your letters. Send my great niece to me. We have lists to make."

"So much for my last quiet day at Persham Abbey with my wife," Lion grumbled to his grandfather an hour later. A footman had just informed him that Lady Harcourt begged his pardon, but she expected to be busy for several hours, as Lady Patricia had sent for Lady Blaine to help her write lists of all the things she might need.

"She is a practical woman, your wife," the earl commented. "She makes a good wife for a campaigning officer and will be an excellent countess."

Lion jutted his chin. "My other grandfather said my mother was like that. Capable, organised, and determined. He said my father's success was at least in part because of my mother."

"No need to bristle at me, my boy," the earl said, peaceably. "I am too old to fight with you even if I wanted to. And I daresay your Grandfather O'Toole was correct. The agents who went to India for me certainly heard excellent reports of your mother. I am sorry you lost her so early, and that I never had the opportunity to know her."

After that comprehensive apology, Lion couldn't keep his hostility at boiling point. In any case, it had more to do with being deprived of his wife than his lingering resentment over his grandfather's lies.

He spent a pleasant hour listening to his grandfather's stories of his father and uncle as children. For the first time, he realised that his grandfather, too, had had a love match. It shone in every word he said about Lady Ruthford. "If she had lived to see her boys grow up, Lion, she would never have allowed me to make the mistakes I made with you. A wonderful woman, my countess. She, too, was a lot like your Dorothea."

After the earl went for his nap, Lion was at a loose end. He found his cousin in the billiards room, idly knocking a few balls around. "Fox. You're up."

"Lion. Where's the little woman? You two are generally joined at the hip."

Lion chuckled. *Not the hip, precisely. But often the same general area.* But Lion wouldn't say that to his cousin. "Ah. Well, as it happens, that ties into the reason I was looking for you. I've had orders from Picton. I'm off to Portugal within the next few days. We are leaving for Newcastle in the morning." He raised his eyes to Heaven, or at least to the ceiling above which his own personal heaven was writing lists. "Dorothea is closeted with Lady Patricia and Lady Blaine planning what she needs to take with her. We're going to be shopping until I leave Newcastle, I fear."

"Good lord, Lion." Fox raised both eyebrows, his lips slightly quirked at one corner. "I never thought to see the great Colonel O'Toole following a woman around like a lap dog. If it is all the same to you, I will wait until the ship is ready to sail before I join you. What ship are we on?"

Lion ignored the jab. Fox could be an ass sometimes. "That's the other thing I needed to say. I'm travelling on a post ship—a sloop called *Augusta*. There won't be accommodations for a lady. We're booking Dorothea on the *Bellflower*, which leaves in a couple of weeks. I want you to escort her."

"Blythe can do that," Fox protested. "I should be back in Portugal with you."

"Blythe is an excellent man, but only a corporal. You have the breeding and the authority to make sure that Lady Harcourt is treated with the courtesy and consideration she deserves. I need you to stay with her, Fox. Don't worry, Gavenor and Cassiday can give me any support I need."

Anger crossed Fox's face so quickly that Lion could not be certain he'd seen it. Especially when Fox gave Lion a jaunty grin. "In that case, Lion, I'd be grateful for the time to see to a few matters I did not think I had time for. If I promise to be there a couple of days before the Bellflower sails, can Lady Harcourt manage? I imagine you will be hiring her a maid."

Fox probably wanted to spend more time with the buxon bar maid he'd been visiting down in the village. No point in reminding Fox that he had a wife. Fox would just say, as he had in London when he'd gone off with a lady of pleasure, that Amelia was in Portugal, and what she did not know would not hurt her. Poor Amelia!

It was none of Lion's business unless it affected Fox's attention to his duty or his behaviour towards Dorothea, and Lion had no complaints on either account.

"I will discuss it with her, old friend, but I'm sure she will have no objection. She is very self sufficient, and the Queen's Head is reputable. I'll talk to grandfather about borrowing the carriage and a couple of footmen until she leaves Newcastle. And perhaps Lady Blaine will know someone who could be a lady's companion for a fortnight."

"My," Fox said. "How will the little dear manage in Portugal if she needs such pampering in England? Are you sure you are wise to take her with you, Lion?"

Fox had been making such remarks for days. Lion had had enough. "Leave it, Fox. Dorothea and I are agreed. She is coming to Portugal. She will have adjustments to make, but she knows that, and I have every confidence in her."

"After—what—twelve days acquaintance? No, no. No need to take offence. I am only joking. I would be happy to squire the lovely Lady Harcourt through a couple of days of shopping in Newcastle, and will make sure she is kept safe on the voyage to Porto."

He bowed deeply enough to make it a mockery. "I daresay you will want me to manage her pin money?"

"Dorothea will manage her own pin money, Fox." Lion trusted his cousin in most things, but money wasn't one of them. "I'll make sure she has enough for the journey, and will leave a letter of credit with my bank in Porto. All you have to do is make sure no one steals from her."

If there was anyone here to wager with, he'd lay odds that Fox would try to touch him for a loan before he left the house tomorrow. He'd say no, of course, as he usually did, but perhaps he should leave a purse with Dorothea to be given to his cousin in Porto. Any earlier, and Fox would gamble it all away again before the *Bellflower* docked in Portugal.

CHAPTER 7

The Earl of Ruthford and Lady Patricia both hugged Dorothea when she and Lion said their farewells. They had come as far as the foyer, but would not go out to the carriage.

"Look after my boy," the earl begged, when Lion hurried outside to make sure all was ready. "Despite the way I treated him, he's made himself into the finest man I know, but he has scars, Dorothea. He has scars—some I put there myself. He will be a great earl with you beside him."

"I know nothing about being a countess," Dorothea protested.

"You know how to love him," said the earl. "That is the best thing an earl—any man—can have. A woman who loves him and believes in him. He will step into my shoes sooner than he would like, but I am not worried for him. Not now that he has you."

She kissed the old man's cheek with tears in her eyes.

She turned to Lady Patricia. Aunt Patricia. The old lady had asked Dorothea to address her in more intimate terms yesterday afternoon, as they went through the still room putting together a medicine chest for Dorothea to take with her.

Aunt Patricia enfolded Dorothea in her arms. "You are a dear girl, Dorothea. Be certain I will look after Persham Abbey for you until you come home to be its mistress."

"I don't wish to take over from you, Aunt Patricia," Dorothea objected, honestly. In fact, she was terrified at the prospect.

"I am more than ready to hand over the reins, my dear," Aunt Patricia insisted. "I am so pleased Lion married you. You are good for Lion and you will be good for the family and our people. Come home while I am still fit to help you make your place here, if you can. You have made a good start, Dorothea. Never doubt it."

"All is ready, my lady," Lion said, passing through the open door with a bounce in his step. "It is time to go." He was so obviously pleased to be on the move that Dorothea felt a surge of pity for the two old people beside her.

The earl lifted a hand in a wave. "Travel safely, do your duty, and come home to us, Lion. I am proud of you, my boy."

Lion gave a short bow. "My lord. Grandfather."

It was the first time Dorothea had heard him use the familial term to the earl, and she was not surprised when the earl's lips quivered before he firmed his mouth and lifted his chin. The gleam of water filming his eyes still gave his emotions away, but all he said was. "I detest goodbyes."

Aunt Patricia surprised everyone in the great entrance hall by putting her arms around Lion, who froze for a moment before returning the embrace. "Be careful, Lion. And take care of Dorothea."

"I will, Aunt," he assured her. He held out a hand to Dorothea, and led her out to the carriage, where Blythe and Lottie were already waiting. Lottie was the maid who had been attending Dorothea. Aunt Patricia insisted on sending her to Newcastle with them until Dorothea had found someone who was prepared to make the journey to Portugal.

Fox wasn't there, nor was he among the outriders who were preparing to escort the carriage. "Does Major Foxton not come with us?" she asked Lion.

"He will meet us in Newcastle later," Lion said. "Or you, at least. He has promised to be there several days before the *Bellflower* sails. He said he had business to attend to. A boxing match or a horse race, I have no doubt, but we don't need him yet, do we, Lady Harcourt?" He always addressed her formally in front of other people, and Dorothea was careful to do likewise, doing her best to hide how inadequate she felt every time she was reminded of their new status.

The presence of the servants prevented Dorothea from doing more than nodding. She didn't say she was very happy to have some more time essentially alone with Lion, for the servants would not demand Lion's attention or sulk because Lion wanted to spend time with Dorothea instead of them.

Nor did she say that a few days without Fox's waspish remarks would be delightful.

It was a full day's journey. They beguiled some of the time with chequers and cards. Lottie, once she got over her awe at being in a carriage with Lord and Lady Harcourt, proved to be something of a chequers champion, but knew no card games. They had taught her several before she admitted that her father had forbidden them in his house as they led to drink, gambling, and the ruin of innocent girls.

"Your father is quite right, if such games are played in riotous places," Dorothea explained. "But a game without wagering, played in private homes or in a private carriage such as this, amongst sober friends is perfectly acceptable even for children, or so my finishing governess told me."

Lottie, whether because she admired Dorothea enormously or because she was really enjoying herself, accepted the rationalisation, and continued to play.

Despite the entertainment and the comfort of the carriage, Dorothea was very pleased when Lion said the next stage was the last before Newcastle. "You will have time for a bath before dinner, Lady Harcourt, if you so wish," he said.

"That will be very pleasant, Lord Harcourt," Dorothea said.

The Queen's Head was pleasant indeed. They had, as requested, set aside a suite of rooms, with a bed chamber, dressing room and sitting room for Dorothea and Lion, and two smaller rooms off the dressing room suitable for servants—or Lion said, for children and their nurses or errant husbands. He went to check on the rest of the party while Dorothea had her bath and came back to report that everyone was satisfied with their accommodations. The footmen were in the servants' quarters upstairs, and the driver, grooms, and outriders above the stables.

Lion came back with a small stack of messages. Appointments for Dorothea. An acknowledgement from Lion's bank manager asking Lion to call at any time convenient to him. Confirmation that cabins had been reserved on the Bellflower for Dorothea's party. A note from the naval officer in charge of the shore station at Tynemouth confirming they had received his letter and would ask the captain of Augusta to make room for him and Blythe on the run to Porto.

"I've ordered dinner served in our room, Lady Harcourt," he told her. "I thought we could send Blythe and Lottie off to their own dinner, and dismiss them for the evening. I will be your maid, and you my valet, if you agree."

Dorothea read the heat in his eyes and nodded, in full agreement with the intention she saw there. Dinner was clearly not the first thing on his mind.

After breakfast the next day, they went their separate ways. "I'll leave the carriage and the footmen with you, my love," Lion told Dorothea. "Take Lottie, as well. I'm going to the docks to check up on the vessels for both of us, and I have some other messages to run, but I hope to be back at the Queen's Head by mid-afternoon. If you are not finished your own errands by then, send a footman with a note to say where you are, and I will join you."

"I might be buying bonnets," Dorothea warned, and he chuckled.

"I am willing to suffer that torture to spend more time with you."

She laughed at that, but he meant it. He had never gone with a woman to buy bonnets and until today he would have said he'd rather face a French charge than suffer through what he imagined the experience to be like. Still, he knew he would be rushing through his own tasks for the day, anxious to join her in hers.

It frightened him sometimes how much he craved her presence; how much he loved her. If she turned from him, it would destroy him.

The harbourmaster was able to tell him where the *Augusta* would dock, and advised him to engage a watcher in Tynemouth to bring him word as soon as the sloop was seen. He gave Lion the name of someone who could be relied on, and Lion wrote the man a note.

Armed with the name of the shipping agent for the *Bellflower*, he went there, next, and was assured Lady Harcourt would be accommodated in the finest available cabin, and treated with the greatest of respect. "It is a very safe ship, my lord," the agent assured him, "and will be part of a convoy with a full naval escort."

His last visit in the area was to the two docks. He came to the one from which Dorothea would embark on the *Bellflower* first. The carriage would be able to bring her nearly to the boat that would take her out to the ship.

He tried to be consoled, but he still hated the idea that he wouldn't be with her every step of the way. All he could do was make it as safe as possible. She would have Fox with her, and he would leave the carriage here for Dorothea's use while she was in Newcastle. The earl's footmen and groom could help guard Dorothea as she crossed the dock.

Further along, and in a seedier area, he found the dock where the *Augusta* would briefly tie up within the next two days. Not a place he wanted Dorothea to come. He would say goodbye at the hotel, then, and make the fifteen-minute walk with his essential kit.

As he headed back into the town, he was deep in thought, but his soldierly instincts had him shifting right even as an assailant rushed out of the shadows of an alley, knife raised. A thump to the back of the man's neck as momentum carried him past disposed of that threat, but two more were close behind him.

I should have worn my sword. Whoever hired them had not paid for the best. The first man had only begun to stir and to groan by the time Lion had laid out another and the third had taken to his heels.

A few dockworkers had stopped to watch, and once the fight was over, two of them offered to take the miscreants to the dock watchman. Accomplices, perhaps. Ready to let them go as soon as Lion was out of sight. He waved the would-be helpers to silence and pulled the first attacker up by his collar.

"Who hired you?"

The man shook his head, and someone said, "Here? What's going on here?"

It was the dock watchman. Lion told him about the attack, breaking off partway through to stomp on the hand of the second man who was reaching for the knife dropped by his accomplice. Once he'd answered all the watchman's questions, and given the man his name and the name of the inn, he left the watchman to the arrest.

"Let me know if you find out who paid them," he asked.

He didn't hold out much hope. The dock watchman seemed a little miffed that he was planning to leave England almost immediately, but the orders of Lion's general took precedence over pursuing charges against some paid bullies. Paid murderers, that was. It wasn't a robbery, whatever the dock watchman thought. All three were intent on doing Lion as much damage as possible.

Westinghouse, probably. Or grandfather's great nephew. I can't think of anyone else in England who wants me dead.

His next errand was to the vicarage of St Nicholas parish church. Quite by chance, while he was passing through the public rooms at the inn last night, he had overheard someone talking about the Bishop of Durham's visit to Newcastle. His Grace was, apparently, staying with Dr Smith, the local vicar.

It was a chance to put into action a plan he had not yet discussed with his wife. He'd thought he'd have to wait until they were together again in Portugal, but if the bishop was willing, Newcastle would be far better.

CHAPTER 8

When Lion rejoined them part way through the afternoon, Dorothea noticed he was favouring one arm and trying to keep his discomfort hidden. She didn't say anything in front of the shoemaker who was currently taking her measurements. On the way to the milliners next door, she did no more than ask him how he was, to which he replied he had had a successful morning and would tell her all about it later.

She assumed he didn't want to discuss whatever had happened in front of the shop servants and other customers, nor the footmen and groom who were carrying her purchases to the carriage, then hurrying back for more.

Instead, she joked he was too early, for she was about to try on hats.

He smiled. "And will look charmingly in them, I am sure. Dorothea, do you have something festive to wear? I have something special in mind for tomorrow. Something festive, and a bonnet to match."

Dorothea's question was naturally, "Where are we going? What sort of festive? I need more information, Lion."

He put a finger on her lips. "It is a secret, but I promise to tell you all about it when we are private." He narrowed his eyes. "There are different kinds of festive?"

"Well, yes. Festive as in a ball?"

He shook his head.

"Festive as in a dinner party on a special occasion?"

Another shake.

Dorothea thought for a moment. "Festive as in a wedding or a christening or a royal garden party."

His face cleared and he nodded. "Yes. That sort of festive." His gaze drifted to the hats, and he suddenly pointed to an absurd concoction of lace, gauze and feathers, with very little actual hat involved. Dorothea had to admit it was pretty, and it was certainly festive. "That would be delightful on you," Lion said.

"His lordship is right," the milliner said. "A perfect festive hat. It would be wasted on a larger woman, but will suit my lady perfectly."

Dorothea demurred. "I have nothing in those colours, Lion."

The milliner, scenting a lucrative sale, immediately offered to have it made up in any colour Dorothea wished, and Dorothea soon found herself sitting in front of the mirror with the whimsy—one could not really describe it as a hat—framing her face.

"I was right, was I not?" Lion said, smugly.

"The blossom-pink dinner gown, my lady?" Lottie suggested. "If you wore it without the cream overskirt, it would be more of an afternoon gown. Perhaps with the oyster linen spencer?"

Yes. That could work. "Something to adjust the neckline," she thought out loud.

"I have gauze in an oyster colour," the milliner offered. "A length of that trimmed with silver lace, folded as a fichu. Then, when I make the hat, I would use the same gauze and lace. I have ribbon in blossom pink and, I think, claret would work to give a little…" she kissed her fingers and made a flinging gesture.

Deciding on the gown and hat for this mystery event wound Dorothea's curiosity up another notch, but she had more hats to order and one more shop to visit before she and Lion could have some time to themselves.

Lion accompanied her even to the haberdasher, where he

showed an interest in gloves, ribbons, stockings, handkerchiefs and pockets. Also, a tendency to double every order she made. He had assured her he was wealthy, but so was Dorothea's father, and he had grumbled and groaned about every item she purchased.

At last, all the shopping was done. Lion still wouldn't talk in the carriage, though he looked as if he was as excited to share the news as she was to hear it. Once they were in their suite, he sent Blythe and Lottie to manage the procession of footmen with packages, telling them to use the door from the inn's passage to the bedchamber. He led Dorothea into the sitting room.

"I've arranged for us to be married again tomorrow," he said.

Dorothea felt her jaw drop and shut it again so she was not staring at him gape mouthed. "Married again?" She had been wondering what it could be for more than an hour, but another wedding had not occurred to her.

"Sit down, my love," he said, "and I shall explain." He sat beside her and put his arm around her.

Lion had been to visit the Bishop of Durham, who happened to be staying with the vicar of St Nicholas Church, which Dorothea could see from the window. He had come away with a common license to marry, dispensation from the bishop for the requirement to wait seven days to use the license, and an appointment with the vicar.

"If anything happens to me, my love, I want you to be able to easily prove that you and I are legally wed. I never want a child of ours to doubt his place in the world or his right to his own name. I had planned to arrange for an army chaplain to wed us again, but this way is better. When I heard the bishop was visiting, I seized my chance. Our chance."

His plan made sense, but only if she was prepared to consider that she might need to prove that her marriage in Scotland was valid, which would only happen if Lion was dead. Her mind recoiled at the thought.

"Do you not like the idea?" Lion sounded anxious. "I do not plan to take silly risks, if that is your concern. But life is uncertain, my darling, and my grandfather's great nephew is in the habit of thinking of the earldom as promised to him. Since I did not know at the time of our first wedding that I was a Strathford-Bowes, he might be able to argue that I gave a false name." He put a caressing hand over the curve of her belly.

"Even now, our child might be growing inside you. Do this to give me peace, Dorothea. Do this for our child."

Put like that, Dorothea could not refuse.

"Of course, I will," she said. "If the bishop does not think it wrong to marry again, then neither do I. I will marry you as often as you wish." She bumped her head into his shoulder, in a surplus of affection, and he winced.

"What has happened?" Dorothea asked.

"A slight strain in my shoulder, dearest. Nothing to worry about," he replied, dropping a kiss on her hair. "I will just have my bath, shall I?"

But while Lottie was dressing Dorothea's hair, she heard Blythe say, "You've bruised your shoulder, Colonel. You should get my lady to rub some of her liniment into that. Going to be a whopping bruise."

Dorothea put up a hand to tell Lottie to stay where she was and tiptoed to the dressing room door, so she could see what her husband was trying to hide from her. A livid bruise about the size of a fist coloured his shoulder.

"I shall get my liniment," she said.

Lion looked over his shoulder. "It is nothing to worry about," he repeated. He submitted to her ministrations, all the while protesting that he hardly felt it at all. "It looks worse than it is." Which wasn't true, for when she asked him to windmill his arm, he was unable to do a full circle.

"You will need to rest it," she scolded him.

He put his other hand on the nape of her neck and encouraged her ear close to his mouth. "You'll have to be on top, then, my love."

Dorothea's cheeks weren't the only part of her that heated, but she didn't allow herself to be distracted. She dropped the subject in front of Blythe, but as soon as they were alone together, she demanded a blow-by-blow account of the attack, and though he didn't quite give her that, he told her enough for her to leap to the conclusion that Westinghouse was seeking revenge. Or the second cousin wished to clear the line of succession.

"Or the villains intended robbery of a wealthy-looking gentleman walking on his own," Lion suggested.

They spoke no more on the topic that evening. Dorothea wanted to explore the wicked suggestion Lion had made earlier, and her questions on the subject ended Lion's interest in dessert. They soon abandoned the sitting room for the bed chamber, leaving various articles of clothing behind them.

B lythe and the Bishop of Durham witnessed their second wedding. Lottie, too. Lion had not been going to invite her, as he thought she was likely to gossip about it back at Persham Abbey, and he didn't want anyone there to question whether they had actually had their wedding in Scotland.

But Dorothea had a different view. "I suggest we tell her what we are doing and why, Lion. Let her talk as much as she likes. If your grandfather's great nephew thinks he can have our marriage declared invalid, he will think again, knowing it was witnessed by the Bishop of Durham.

The vicar performed the service, adapting the words in places to acknowledge their previous vows. The ceremony was far less perfunctory than the one over the anvil, and the medieval church was indescribably more magnificent. Dorothea would remember the hurried wedding in Scotland with wistful affection, for it marked the start of her life with Lion, but this time felt just as significant, for it signified Lion's love for her.

Afterwards, Blythe walked back to the hotel with Lottie. Dorothea and Lion had ices and then strolled around the town.

Dorothea had made no other plans for the day. "Any other fittings can wait," she said. "I wanted to spend today with you, for it might be the last time for weeks. I want it to be all about us, with no business."

She mostly got her wish, though the manager approached them as soon as they arrived back at the Queen's Head. "Lord Harcourt, there is a female here who insists you will want to see her. She says the harbourmaster sent her."

Said female proved to be Emily Parker, wife of Sergeant John Parker of the 97th Foot. A woman in her middle years, she had been in England for a year, seeing the Parker offspring settled.

"I am meant to be joining my husband, my lady," she told Dorothea when Lion called his wife over to join them. "The passage is more expensive than I expected, and the cost of staying in Newcastle until the ship arrives… Well. The harbourmaster said Lord Harcourt asked to be told about any respectable women who wanted to travel to Portugal because Lady Harcourt would need a maid and female companion for the journey. I thought I would not wait lest he found someone else, so I came straight away to ask if I might do."

Lion seemed satisfied with the woman. Dorothea asked Mrs Parker about the children she had come home for. Her rather plain face lit up as she explained she had brought them to family for their final years of education. She talked about Jack, who had followed his father into the 97th Foot, Meggie, who had just married a haberdasher in Durham, and young Tom, who was very clever, and was a scholarship student in Edinburgh, studying divinities.

"Have you ever been a maid, Mrs Parker?" Dorothea asked.

Mrs Parker pressed her lips together then bit the upper one. "I must tell you, I have no experience as a maid, but I am willing and used to turning my hand to whatever is needed, and I do not get seasick, which must be an advantage."

Dorothea agreed. She said, "I need female companionship more than I need someone to dress my hair. Also, Mrs Parker, I appreciate honesty and initiative. You have shown both. Lion, unless you have an objection, I would like to send Lottie home, and have Mrs Parker move in with me, as soon as you leave."

The relief on Mrs Parker's face spoke volumes about her financial concerns. Lion must have realised that, too, for he said, "We will pay your passage, accommodation, and food, Mrs Parker, and a wage of two guineas a month. If that is acceptable, you can start tomorrow. If you do not have accommodation, I shall arrange a room for you here. Dorothea, I suggest we keep Lottie and send her home with the carriage after you are gone. You will need the carriage while you remain in Newcastle, and I shall feel happier if you have Grandfather's men on hand, at least until Fox joins you."

That was only the first of the interruptions to Dorothea's business-free day. The magistrate arrived next, and Lion spent more than half an hour with him, answering his questions about the assault. The third interruption was the message Lion received with his dinner. The *Augusta* had docked and would sail the following afternoon. Lion must be aboard by midday.

CHAPTER 9

Dorothea had the courage of a soldier's wife. She made no complaint when he read her the note from the harbourmaster. "Blythe will need to be told so he can pack for you," she said. "Is there anything you need me to do to ease your departure, Lion?"

She had already done it—not just with her calm acceptance but by holding in check by force of her will the tears that were very close to the surface. She would weep for him when he was gone; of that, he had no doubt. And dog that he was, he rejoiced that she would miss him even as he was thankful to her for sparing him her tears.

For now, though, he was still here. "Let us have an early night, my love," he suggested.

"With little enough sleep, I hope," she retorted, to the delight of his heart.

They were both heavy eyed in the morning, though more from the sorrow of parting than from the tempestuous night, during which they had slept in one another's arms for brief respites between passion.

Dorothea had come close to losing her temper when he told her he planned to walk to the docks so she could have the use of the carriage. "After the attack on you just two days ago?" she demanded.

"Which failed," he pointed out.

"I do not see the need to give them another opportunity," she snapped back. She calmed herself and turned cajoling. "Please, Lion, take the carriage and the footmen. I shall wait here in the hotel. In my room, even. I shall not venture out until they return to escort me."

In the end, to give her comfort, he agreed, and sent Blythe to order the carriage prepared. Mrs Parker whisked off into the dressing room, leaving him and Dorothea alone to make their farewells.

"It shall be two weeks, or a bit more," Dorothea said, smiling even as her eyes glistened with unshed tears. "We will be together again, and in the meantime, I mean to learn everything I can about being an army wife from Mrs Parker, who has followed the drum for twenty years, since she was no older than me, Lion." Mrs Parker was a sergeant's wife, which was different. But Dorothea would learn quickly, Lion had no doubt.

"She will leave you at Porto," Lion reminded her, "but I shall bring you someone else. One of the officer's wives."

"I am not helpless, Lion. I have had most of my jumps and many of my dresses designed so I can get into them myself."

He rubbed his forefinger under her chin. "But think of my consequence, dearest heart. The colonel's wife to be unattended? Not to be thought of."

"As long as I have as much of you as the army can spare, I need nothing else, my love," she assured him, throwing her arms around him and hugging him tight.

He hugged her back, then put her a little way from him so that he could pull his gift for her from an inner pocket of his coat. It was a square of silk dyed in a rainbow of colours—the centre a paisley of red and gold on a royal blue field, the border a deeper blue with a row of white embroidered elephants, richly caparisoned in red and gold, parading trunk to tail in an endless march around the edge, just above the knotted fringe. A handkerchief, he had always thought it, though he had never used it as one.

"This was my mother's, my love. One of the few things I have of hers. She tucked it into my shirt the last time I saw her, and it has never left my possession."

Dorothea tried to give it back, but he insisted she keep it. "You are mine and I am yours," he told her, "and the handkerchief will be a link between us. A token of how much I love you. You are mine, and therefore if it is with you, so am I."

She nodded, the tears overflowing, and so he kissed her to stop her crying, for it tore his heart out to leave her distressed. She must have known, for when the knock came at the door and Blythe's voice called out that the coach was ready, she stepped back, composed again.

"I shall treasure the handkerchief for your mother's sake, Lion, as well as yours," she said. "Now go and do your duty. I shall be with you soon."

He was tempted to repeat all the warnings he'd given her about going nowhere without a footman, her companion and preferably Fox, too, in attendance, and staying out of the way of the sailors on the ship. But he had said it all, and she was right. He had to go.

"I love you, Dorothea." That, at least, could not be repeated too many times.

"I love you, Lion," she replied.

His last sight of her was when he looked back through the carriage window. She was at the window of their little sitting room, one hand raised in a wave. "I love you," he mouthed again.

He should be glad to be going back to the life that was all he had known for most of his life. The army. The cavalry, to be more specific. Always surrounded and yet always alone. Friendly with his men, but unable to share with them. Because he was different from them. Because he bore the responsibility of command. Because, before Dorothea, he had not allowed anyone close enough to hurt him since all of his close family had died one after another and he had been sent to cold disapproving strangers in England.

Except, for his cousin Fox, his first friend in England. Even Fox had been separated from him when he climbed the ranks more swiftly than his cousin. He could no longer confide everything in his friend, for it would not be fair to his other officers, and Lion was, first and foremost, a soldier.

And yet, he could not remain a soldier. Not for long. For the first time, he could consider that truth without despair. It would be change, but perhaps it would not be terrible. He had a reason to look beyond life in the cavalry to something new. Not the title, though he hoped he would do it justice. Not even peace, which he yearned for. But Dorothea. Yes, and every child they made together.

Men rushed on and off the *Augusta*. Sailors, all business. Dockhands, loading things into the hold. Lion, with Blythe carrying his trunk, asked at the gangplank for the captain.

"On the bridge, sir," said the officer who had barred their way. A fresh-faced boy, he was. They started them young in the navy. "Are you Colonel O'Toole, sir?"

Lion confirmed his identity and was waved aboard. "Ask anyone for the officer's mess, sir," the boy said. "Your man can stow your things wherever he can find space out of the way. We'll sort it out once we are underway."

Blythe sought directions and disappeared with the trunk, while Lion climbed the steps to the bridge, stepping back several times to avoid the rushing dockhands.

He had almost reached the ladder up to the deck when he felt hands giving him a hard shove towards the rail. He lost his balance, but twisted and grabbed one of the arms that had pushed him, pulling on it to right himself even as he stepped out of the way of the dockhand whose momentum carried him on and over the rail.

A splash announced the assailant's arrival in the river.

Lion straightened his coat and continued on up the ladder, ignoring the shouts and splashes from the water and the stares of sailors and dockhands.

The captain waited him with a raised eyebrow. "Someone thought to give you a bath, Colonel O'Toole? I take it you are Colonel O'Toole."

"I am," Lion agreed. "And yes. That man is taking the dunking he intended for me. I am not sure why. I can swim—which is more than can be said for my attacker."

"Yes," the captain acknowledged. "I saw the shove. One of my men has tossed him a line. If you want to find out why, you can talk to him later. He has just earned himself a career in His Majesty's Navy. I don't have time to involve the watchman, and I cannot just leave him to run around pushing people overboard. He'll be in the brig when you want him, and will stay there until you are off my ship."

Roderick again. Or the cousin. Lion would ask, but he doubted the man knew anything. The others hadn't. The magistrate had been given a general description of their paymaster, but all that was certain was his height. A tall man. Even the impression of bulk, which fitted Roderick, could be feigned with a pillow or extra wrappings. They'd agreed the man was gentry, though he'd attempted to disguise his accent, but that still left the field open if it was even true.

Lion hoped that the attacks would cease now he was leaving England. At least in Portugal, most of the enemy wore another uniform.

⁂

Dorothea sent one of the footmen down to the stables with a message to be given to the driver as soon as he arrived back from the docks. She instructed her maid and her companion to dress for a carriage ride. No doubt Lion would not see her, and would not be able to recognise her in the distance if he did, but she was going to Tynemouth to watch her husband's ship until it was out of sight.

It was windy, with gusts of rain, but she saw the little vessel coming, and stood silently beside the carriage, watching it until it disappeared out to sea, taking Lion away.

It was her only outing that day. All the next day, too, she remained in her hotel apartment and moped. Neither Lizzie nor Mrs Parker said a word. Lizzie watched her with concern and whispered to Mrs Parker, "She misses him enormously, Mrs Parker. It is so romantic."

Mrs Parker's glance held more than a hint of contempt. "She will need to be tougher than this to survive a campaign," she whispered back.

It was the spur Dorothea needed, for the experienced army wife was correct. She would continue to feel the absence of her husband with every fibre. She could do nothing about that. But she did not need to let it show.

She waited a few minutes so that they would not realise she had heard them, then asked Lizzie to send a footman to summon the carriage. "I have been making up a medicine chest to take with me to Portugal, and I have a list of items that I need to add to it. Ask the innkeeper or his wife for directions to a respectable apothecary, if you would, please."

She turned to her new companion. "Emily, the chest is in my dressing room. I would appreciate your opinion, and any suggestions for additional supplies."

In the next few days, Dorothea discovered the value of keeping busy. She also discovered that Emily, while willing enough, was not as useful as she had hoped. She knew the army well, but from the perspective of the ranks.

Asked about the duties of officers' wives, she said, "They don't have duties, Lady Harcourt. Or, at least, not any that are useful to the army. They mostly remain in England, but those who do follow their husbands stay at headquarters, or some other place well back from the lines and hold dances and dinner parties and such like."

So much for that. Lion had mentioned Fox's wife, Amelia, who did travel with Lion and his men. Dorothea would have to wait and talk to her.

Emily was more helpful when it came to supplies. She approved of most of Dorothea's purchases, but pointed out anything that would be awkward to launder, or that would not work in the field. Boots, for example, that would hurt the feet after an hour of slogging through mud. "You might expect to always be on horseback or in a carriage, but carriages bog down and horses go lame," she instructed. It was all very useful.

It was a pity Emily was not better company. Dorothea supposed being so much older partially excused the slight condescension with which she delivered every piece of advice, but that didn't prevent Dorothea from finding it annoying.

Dorothea had asked her companion to call her by her first name, but Emily had been horrified. "It would not be right, my lady. You are a viscountess and a colonel's wife," she had pointed out. So that was that.

Dorothea was lonely, though she had spent most of her life keeping herself company and had been content. It was ridiculous, but after less than a fortnight of spending nearly every waking hour with Lion, she was out of the habit. However, as Edith had so unkindly pointed out, she would have to expect more of this in her future.

You must be worthy of Lion, Dorothea, she scolded herself. *You insisted on following him to Portugal. You told him you would not be a burden.* Perhaps she had been wrong. She foresaw many more lonely days and nights in her future. Perhaps, after all, she should remain in England and learn how to be a countess.

She shuddered. *Be the kind of wife that Emily despises, who lives her own life far from her husband?*

No. Lion was not just her husband and her lover. He was her friend. He paid her the enormous compliment of respecting her. And she did not think she was deluding herself in believing that she could be of use to him.

Blythe would make sure he was fed and dressed, and had a place to lay his head at night. Lion's other officers would make sure that his orders were followed. However, there were other things only she could do. She could bring him the peace that he said he found in her arms. She could listen to his personal concerns, about his family and his duties.

Perhaps she did not know how to be the colonel's lady, but she would learn. Certainly, she had no idea how to be the earl's countess, but she would learn that, too.

Dorothea Brabant had dreamed of a simple life with a man of her own class. Dorothea O'Toole had thought her happiness might come from following the drum with the man she had come to love. Dorothea Strathford-Bowes would find her destiny side by side with her husband, wherever that might lead her.

Meanwhile, she slept with her hand on his mother's handkerchief, which spent each night under her pillow.

Lion made a swift journey to Portugal, and another from Porto to the Marquess of Wellington's headquarters in Freineda. Nine days after he left Newcastle, Lion was back with his men, if just for the night. Apart from an unsuccessful sniper attack as he travelled a lonely portion of the road, the journey had been uneventful. He'd report to Picton in Freineda the next day.

He spent the evening with his two senior officers, receiving their reports. As always in winter quarters, Major Michael Cassiday's main problems had centred around keeping the men—and the camp followers who supported them—from deteriorating into a bored rabble. He'd had the dragoons out training in all weathers, which kept them from having the energy to do more than grumble, but he reported a raft of minor problems amongst the civilians. The farrier was having an affair with the suttler's wife. The women as a body had refused to do any laundry for one of the troop captains and would not say why. One of the troopers had two of the women fighting over him and refused to choose one or the other.

Captain Hugh Gavenor, the leader of Lion's exploring officers, was more reticent. Bear, they called him. A name that had attached to him in childhood because he was so big, and one of the reasons that the cadre of exploring officers under Lion's command had been dubbed Lion's Zoo by the wits of the regiment.

He claimed no particular problems, but as Lion was about to dismiss them both so he could get some sleep before the morning's trip to Freineda, he said, "Colonel? Could I have a moment on a personal matter? It is somewhat urgent."

Something in Bear's usually impassive face set alarm bells ringing. "Of course. I'll walk you back towards your tent."

Lion waited until they were well away from any tents and any people before he said, "Is there something wrong?"

Bear grimaced. "There is. The information leaks, Lion. They stopped after we discovered what the Greek female and her uncle were up to."

Lion nodded. The Nomikos uncle and niece had convinced Lion they were fighting for Greek independence. To damage the French was to damage the Turk's, the occupiers of their homeland. Instead, they were selling secrets to the French—mainly news about the movements of Lion and his men. They had fled before they could be apprehended and shot.

"The leaks started up again just after Christmas," Bear said.

Bear had not said anything Lion didn't know. "Someone else was working with them," he agreed.

"They have stopped again, Lion." Bear said. "Perhaps whoever it was has left Portugal."

Lion stopped walking as he absorbed that. "You think *I* am betraying England and our men?"

Bear shook his head. "On the contrary. I trust you, Lion. Nobody else."

"Fox and Cassiday can be trusted"

Bear shrugged. "I hope so. Just in case, watch your back, Lion. And have alternate plans others do not know for everything they do know."

The worst of it was that Lion could not dismiss the warning. Too many lives depended on him being right. But surely Bear must be wrong, for all of his officers were Englishmen and patriots. Weren't they?

When Lion reported to General Picton, he was greeted with an irascable, "Colonel O'Toole, deigning to take a break from raping merchants' daughters in order to fight a war." Several of the officers clustered around him smiled and one snickered.

Lion reined in his angry response. One did not punch one's general. "Sir, whoever told you that I raped anyone is a liar."

The officers looked between the pair of them like people at a tennis match.

Picton raised his eyebrows. "Do you deny that you were forced to marry the Brabant heroine after abducting her?"

"I do, sir," he replied. "My lady wife was abducted, but not by me. We chose to marry, and I will be pleased to make you known to her when she arrives in Portugal."

Picton puffed out his chest. "I'll have you know, O'Toole, that my information comes from none other than the woman's jilted betrothed."

That explained a few things. "Roderick Westinghouse, general?"

The general nodded.

"Westinghouse is not only a liar, sir. He is also a fool if he expects such slurs to withstand my arrival in Portugal with the truth. My wife refused his suit, repeatedly, so he abducted her. He was about to assault her in the cruellest and most intimate of ways when she hit him over the head with a chamber pot and laid him out. Aided, I might add, by his state of inebriation. It was my good fortune to be in the right place to offer her some small assistance. We decided we would suit, and we married. We have the approval of her father and my grandfather."

Picton snorted. "Fine speaking."

"Undoubtedly, sir, gossip from England will arrive to confirm my report of the matter. Certainly, my wife will be here within the fortnight if you wish to talk to her privately and hear her side. I came as fast as I could on your orders, but she follows on the next available merchant ship."

Picton still looked doubtful, but he left the matter in preference for briefing his officers. Since the general had been in England for several months, his briefing added little to the information Lion already had. However, one's general must be obeyed. Lion listened without comment.

Later, after the meeting, one of the other officers walked out with him. "Westinghouse is staying with a local nobressza, the Conde de Estombar. Westinghouse has been painting you in the harshest colours all over the British army. No one can see why an heiress, even a merchant's daughter, would prefer a career military officer to the probable heir to an earldom. No one who hasn't met any of the Westinghouse brothers, that is. Pompous windbags, and nasty with it."

Lion thanked him. He wondered if there was any point in advertising that *he* was an earl's heir. On the other hand, saying so would cast Dorothea in a bad light, totally unwarranted. He would leave things be and simply tell the truth. In time, the rumours would be replaced with something else.

CHAPTER 10

Dorothea looked around the cabin she had shared with Emily. It had been very comfortable, though not the trip with her husband that she'd hoped for.

Without consciously meaning to do so, she put her hand through the slit in the seam of her skirt, and into the pocket she wore around her waist to stroke the handkerchief Lion had given her to remember him by. It had been a great comfort to her since he had kissed her goodbye. Still, she would be with him soon.

The very thought of him brought a smile to her face and then a frown. "You are thinking of your husband, my lady," Emily guessed.

"I am hoping the colonel will be pleased to see me," Dorothea admitted. In their marriage so far, they had been apart for longer than they had been together.

"Of course, he will." Emily sounded confident. "You are newly weds, are you not?"

That, of course, was precisely the problem. They had known one another three days when they were wed. They had had ten more days together as husband and wife.

"I have shared a room with you for longer than I have shared one with my husband," Dorothea told Emily. Ten nights in

Newcastle and seven on the ocean. But at last they were setting anchor in Porto, and soon she and Lion would be back together again.

The weeks apart had only strengthened and deepened Dorothea's love for her husband, but she had had little to do except think of him, ask Fox for stories about him, and wonder about her life with him. Lion had been busy preparing for his troops for the invasion of Spain. Would he have spared any thought at all for the wife he had taken out of pity?

For surely the love he declared in the heat of passion would have cooled while they were apart. What did a girl like Dorothea have to offer a man of his years, experience, and noble birth?

Certainly, Fox thought Lion's marriage was a mistake. Not that he actually said so. He was charming and friendly, and a great admirer of Lion.

His stories in praise of Lion, though, always seemed to have a sting in them, presenting Lion as someone who moved from woman to woman, whose temper was uncontrolled and brutal, who had no close friends apart from Fox himself, who was ruthless and some-times cruel. The Lion he spoke of was not the Lion she thought she knew. Somehow, she always came away from a conversation with Fox feeling less sure of herself.

Someone knocked on the door, and Emily opened it. Fox saun-tered in, and a couple of sailors peered into the room. "These men have come to carry your trunks, ladies, and I am here to escort you up on deck. The captain wants to send you ashore in the first boat."

Emily scurried past him with her bag. She was skittish around Fox. Dorothea could not tell whether she had something against the man, or whether it was just that he was a major, and her husband only a sergeant. Emily would not say.

Dorothea went to pick up her own bag, but Fox was before her. He hefted it easily, and gestured for her to precede him. She certainly could not fault his care and concern, as he helped her into the sling the sailors had prepared to lower her into the row boat. Emily was already waiting. She had refused to be treated like luggage and climbed down the rope ladder. Next time, Dorothea was going to do that.

She took her seat on the bench next to Emily, her eyes searching ahead of her for her first sight of Lion. The town of Porto climbed a hill in the sun, terrace after terrace of multi-storied buildings with red tiled roofs and walls bright white in the sun or washed with soft hues of yellow, blue or orange. A fringe of steeple, towers and domes stretched into the sky from the hilltops. At the river's edge, a long quay drew nearer with every stroke, with the city walls that backed it slowly cutting off her view of the town as the boat surged closer.

Splashes of colour resolved into figures as they approached— mostly men, many in uniform. None of them were Lion.

When they pulled alongside a stone slope that led from the water up to the quay, she still had not seen him. Fox handed her ashore. "Have a care, Dorothea. The slope is slippery," he warned. "Hold on to me."

He covered her hand on his arm with his own as he escorted her up above the tide level. Once her footing was stable, she disengaged and hurried ahead, only to be disappointed when she reached the little group who waited at the top, none of whom were Lion, all of whom were strangers.

The woman who shrieked and launched herself at Fox must be Fox's wife Amelia. Or, given the way Fox was kissing her, Dorothea hoped so. Emily was also in an embrace. Two of their party of three had been greeted by their spouse.

A man approached her, an officer by the gilt on his uniform. "Lady Harcourt, I am Michael Cassidy. I bring your husband's apologies. He was called to headquarters, so he sent me to bring you to our winter camp."

Dorothea fought back her disappointment, and gave him her hand in greeting. He bent over it and kissed the air above her glove.

Lion had told Dorothea about Major Michael Cassiday, and so had Fox. Fox was in charge of one of Lion's two squadrons of dragoons and Major Cassiday of the other, though Fox thought he was a little young for the responsibility. "He's well known for his success with the ladies, Dorothea. Though I'm sure he will not try his charms on you. You are Lion's wife, after all."

Dorothea examined the man with a critical eye. He was, she thought, a handsome man. Not to her taste, it went without saying. Indeed, in all but height, he was Lion's opposite. Straight hair so fair as to be nearly white rather than Lion's dark curls. Light blue eyes rather than a brown so dark it appeared black. Sparse sandy eyebrows, instead of thick, black, and emphatic. He was grinning at her, his expression open, friendly, and full of good humour.

"Will I pass muster, Lady Harcourt?"

Dorothea blushed. "I beg your pardon. I did not mean to stare. Both Lion and Fox have spoken of you, Major Cassiday. It is nice to meet you."

Fox had joined them, his wife at his side. He greeted his colleague with a nod and a brief. "Cassiday."

"Foxton," Cassiday replied.

"My lady," Fox said, "may I be permitted to present my wife, Amelia? Amelia, Lady Harcourt."

"It is nice to meet you, Mrs Foxton," Dorothea said.

Fox's wife was a beauty of the kind often called an English rose: golden curls, wide blue eyes, and a peaches and cream complexion protected by a wide-brimmed hat.

She bobbed a curtsey. "You can call me Amelia, my lady," she said. Her voice was carefully refined. "I am pleased to meet you, too. All of the wives will be jealous I met you first. We couldn't believe it when the colonel said he married while he was in England. The colonel asked me to come, my lady. He said your maid for the journey would not be coming on to camp with you, and I should help out until you make other arrangements." She smiled anxiously, nodding as if to encourage Dorothea's agreement.

Help out? "As my maid, you mean?" Dorothea asked. "But you are a major's wife, not a servant."

She glanced at Fox. He was glowering at his wife, but the expression he turned on Dorothea was all smiles. "As your companion, if you will, my lady. But Amelia does not mind serving you. This is the army, Lady Harcourt. We all must turn our hand to whatever needs to be done. Amelia would be pleased to be your lady in waiting, won't you, darling."

Amelia chuckled. "Lady in waiting! Get along with you, Major Foxton."

"If you are not too tired, my lady," Cassiday said, "I have a carriage waiting. We can make Lordelo tonight if we leave now."

Dorothea looked around for her trunks. "Of course. I am ready now, Major. Is my husband in Lordelo?"

"Lord, no, my lady," Cassiday replied. "We're camped outside of Almeida. If the weather holds, we should be there in five or six days. But you needn't worry. I have arranged respectable places for you to stay, and you shall have Mrs Foxton's company to give you countenance."

He misunderstood the reason for her sudden distress. Five days! Perhaps even another week or more!

Lion must do his duty, she scolded herself. *And you must not make a fuss.* Through the slit in the side of her skirt, she stroked her fingers over the handkerchief.

⁂

A week after Lion's arrival in Freineda, he began asking for permission to return to his men. And, incidentally, his wife. The drive into Spain should have started on the 1st of June, but the rains had not come, meaning insufficient feed for the horses along the way. An army could not march without its horses.

Also, Wellington was waiting on pontoons to cross the rivers they would encounter along the way. The pontoons had been ordered months ago, and were late, so the marquess was irritated and not inclined to let Lion go.

Lion asked again the next day. He had his orders for the men under his command. Both of his squadrons would be fighting in the army of General Picton. The exploring officers, the soldiers others called his Zoo, were already in the field. His men needed him.

Furthermore, he didn't want to be in the vicinity of the

scoundrel who apparently still wanted his wife. Westinghouse was welcomed everywhere. He was always accompanied by the Conde, his host, and sat glowering at Lion whenever they were in the same room.

Then the news of Lion's legitimate birth and subsequent title arrived by post from England, as expected. Less expected were the mostly accurate accounts of Westinghouse's abduction of Dorothea, her subsequent rescue, and her marriage to Lion. This story was usually given the most romantic of glosses—Lion saw the fine hand of Lady Blaine and her network of correspondents.

After that, Westinghouse stopped appearing in public, and most of Lion's fellow officers took him to one side to tell him they had always believed in him.

Days more passed before he was finally given his release. In Portugal's mountains, the twenty miles to Almeida took half a day, but Lion was spurred on by the hope his wife would be waiting for him.

His men were camped outside the fortified village. Many village buildings had been badly damaged when stored gunpowder blew up during an attack some four years ago, so quartering even his officers on the villagers had not been an option and the barracks within the fortifications were already occupied.

Lion rode through the camp, waving to his men. No sign of Fox or Michael Cassiday. He dismounted at the farmhouse he had rented, leaving his horse to one of his men, and hurrying inside.

A shout brought Blythe running. "Colonel! Sir!"

"Any word from Lady Harcourt, Blythe?" Lion asked.

Blythe beamed. "Message from Major Cassiday, sir. My lord. Messenger said they should be here tomorrow."

Lion took the package Blythe handed him and smiled fondly at the note written in Dorothea's hand. Realising he was being watched, he wiped the smile from his face and tucked the note inside his jacket to read when he was alone. He opened the report. *Today's date. Michael's signature.* Lady Harcourt was well. Her ship had been delayed by a storm and had arrived two days late, so they had left Porto immediately. Michael planned to stop in Almendra for the night.

Lion checked his pocket watch. The fifteen-hour days of June gave him more than enough time to reach that village before nightfall. "Blythe, have another horse saddled for me, and tell the duty officer that I want a platoon to ride with me to Almendra to meet up with my wife. Then come and help me find a clean shirt to put on to welcome her."

CHAPTER 11

Fox meant well, Dorothea supposed, but remarks he presumably intended to be encouraging left her with more and more doubts. He had been making them since he joined her and Emily in Newcastle, continued throughout the voyage, and now inserted them into the journey through Portugal.

"You mustn't suppose that Lion's failure to meet you means he doesn't want you," he assured her. "He must do his duty, you know. And the regiment has always been more important to him than any family ties."

"I am sure it won't matter to Lion that you come from a common family. Of course, now he is to be earl, he does not need your dowry any more. It is just as well that you and he have a love match, Dorothea. And if he tires of you, at least you will be a countess."

"You mustn't worry about how to go on, Dorothea. Most of the senior officers are from the aristocratic families, but you can always ask me if you are afraid of doing something wrong."

And the comments that repeated in her mind most stridently; the ones that echoed her own fears. "Take no notice of what the officers' wives say about your origins. Once they see that you are nearly as ladylike as someone born to our own class, I am sure they will accept you."

He was Lion's cousin, so of course he wanted to help her. But she wished he was not so good at holding up a mirror to all her faults.

The tensions between Michael and Fox made Dorothea uncomfortable, too. On Fox's part, they consisted of ambiguous remarks that never failed to disturb Michael's usually equitable temper, without being so openly insulting that he was justified in taking exception. Michael responded with a formal and distant courtesy, officer to officer, that contrasted sharply with the growing warmth between Dorothea and Amelia.

They stayed at nights in a variety of places. Pousadas, which was what the Portuguese called their inns, convents and, once, a private home. Dorothea was grateful Lion had thought to send Amelia to her, for it would have been even more daunting without a female companion. Amelia was a blessing—a practical woman with a warm and open nature, who was delighted to discover that the wife of her adored husband's superior officer was willing to be friends.

She made no bones about the fact that she came from peasant stock—her grandfather was a tenant farmer, and her father a younger son who had taken the King's shilling and risen through the ranks to become sergeant. At first, she was inclined to be in awe of Dorothea, who was a viscountess and doomed to become a countess when Lion succeeded to the title. But her reserve soon wore off, and she was full of practical advice about ways a woman could ease the difficulties of travelling behind the army.

Dorothea did notice that her anecdotes and information all came from her girlhood at her mother's side. Asked about the duties of an officer's wife, she said, "Major Foxton does not like me to do anything except cook for him and keep our room clean." She blushed. "Ladies do not work, he tells me."

Since she had been raised to manage a household, Dorothea protested. "Ladies work very hard, Amelia. They supervise their servants, look after their stillrooms, sew decorative items for their houses, organise charitable activities to look after their villagers and those who have met with misfortune."

"I do not have any of those, Dorothea," Amelia pointed out. Dorothea had insisted on being on first-name terms with Lion's cousin and his wife, and had included the charming Major Cassiday in the privilege of friendship.

Fox, Dorothea was fast realising, treated his wife with barely veiled disdain, even as he corrected every word or action that he considered might draw attention to her lowly birth. Dorothea was finding it harder by the day to like her husband's closest friend.

It was a long and gruelling journey, the hours of idleness on rough roads in the swaying carriage relieved only when the two women had to walk up or down a steep slope to spare the horses, or cross a river on a boat with the carriage precariously tied to another. Portugal seemed to comprise nothing but mountains, rivers, and dust. Dorothea ended each day tired to the bone.

Then, however, they made their last night time stop of the journey, and Lion was waiting. She ran into his arms, lifted her face for his enthusiastic kiss, and felt her uncertainties and troubles melt away. Suddenly, she was not tired at all.

"I will be your maid," he said as soon as he had escorted her to the room set aside for her, and sent Amelia to Fox. They did not join the others for dinner, and in Lion's arms, Dorothea could not doubt his love, or her own.

On the next day, they had several streams and a river to cross. It was a much better day than those before them. Lion took her up in front of him on his horse for part of the day. "Fox says he does not know how I shall manage since I am not a good rider," Dorothea admitted. "I am determined to continue practicing, Lion. This is a much better way to travel than in the carriage."

"I shall be pleased to ride with you when I can, my love," Lion assured her. "I warn you, though, you will be glad of the carriage when it rains, or when you cannot otherwise get out of the army's dust. I'm glad Michael found you one with good springs."

Dorothea was surprised. "It is mine? My carriage?"

"Yes, indeed. The colonel's wife needs her own carriage. Her own servant, too."

"It was kind of Amelia to keep me company on the journey, and kind of you to suggest it. It seems wrong, though, for a major's wife to be my servant, for all that Fox calls her my lady in waiting."

"Was there a question, there, my wife? Yes, Amelia is not gentry-born. Fox can be sensitive about it, at times."

"Neither am I gentry born," Dorothea pointed out. "I like Amelia. She is sweet and kind, and she adores Fox."

"She is an innocent," Lion told her, "for all she has followed the army all her life. I told Fox, when he started paying attention to her, that if he gave her expectations or went beyond flirting, he would have to marry her, and he did. Just as well, for her father would have shot him, and then I would have had to hang the sergeant, and I would be down two good men."

He laughed, so he was joking. Dorothea hoped he was joking. Amelia had told Dorothea all about her origins, but not that Fox had been forced to marry her. Dorothea hoped she didn't know. Poor Amelia!

Lion told her that news of his change in surname and status had reached headquarters and his own men. "I've told them I will remain Colonel O'Toole for the duration of the war, Dorothea. The men are used to it. I hope you don't mind. They can, of course, call you Lady Harcourt."

She eyed his chin, contemplating a kiss but deciding that the horse was so bouncy and the ground so uneven she might bruise it instead of caress it. "I am Mrs O'Toole, of course. I was that first, in any case."

The sun was nearly at the horizon when they rode into the camp of the 25th Dragoons. All around, men stopped what they were doing to salute their colonel and stare at his wife. They had a house, Lion had told her—a farmhouse just outside of the village and on the edge of the camp.

"We will share it with Fox and Amelia, Blythe, and Michael and… and Michael."

Michael and whom, Dorothea wondered. What would Lion not

want to tell her? "Does Michael have a mistress, Lion? Does she live with us?"

"I shall tell him he has to find Bianca another place to live," Lion offered.

"No, Lion. That is not necessary. I am not a hypocrite to blame another woman for doing what might have been forced on me. Let Bianca stay with Michael. I am sure she must be very nice."

Lion's brow creased as he thought about it.

"Do Bianca and Amelia follow the army when you invade, Lion?" Dorothea asked.

"Yes, they do."

"Then Bianca must be allowed to stay. She and Amelia and I shall be friends, lest we cause unrest between you and your squadron majors, Lion."

He must have agreed with her, for he dropped the subject as he halted in front of a single-story stone building, low to the ground, with a tiled roof. "Home, Lady Harcourt. At least for a week or two, until we begin the advance."

It proved to contain a room for living and also cooking. The large open fireplace at one end of the room held several three-legged copper pots. On the long wall opposite the door, a stone bench surrounded by colourful tiles functioned as a scullery, given the bowls and buckets that sat on or under it. The table—a huge solid slab, like a kitchen table in any substantial house in England, was both work surface and dining space.

The big room took up around half of the floor space of the building. The rest was three bedchambers, one at the fireplace end of the living room, and two at the other. Another tiny bedroom was in a lean-to porch beyond the back door. Lion showed her around, and they were all very plain, except for a brightly striped blanket across the bed in one room and the dress uniforms and women's dresses that hung on pegs in two of the rooms.

Corporal Blythe and a couple of other soldiers carried Dorothea's trunks and her bag into the one bedchamber without women's dresses. The largest room that shared a wall with the fire-place, which she supposed went with being a colonel. And with the largest bed. Dorothea had plans for that bed, after riding with Lion for most of the day, pressed up against his broad back.

"Lion," said Michael Cassiday from the door, "The scouts are back. Bear asked me to fetch you to hear their report."

Lion took Dorothea's hands. "I have to go," he said. "I'll be back as soon as I can."

In moments, all of the soldiers were gone, and Dorothea was alone in her new home.

But only for a moment. Amelia came in, another woman behind her. The second woman's dark curls and sun-kissed skin marked her as Spanish or Portuguese as much as her clothing—a white blouse with voluminous sleeves under a red shawl that crossed over at the front with the ends tucked into the waist of her green skirt.

Amelia didn't offer to introduce her. "Lady Harcourt, shall I unpack your bag?" she asked. Her cheeks coloured. "Dorothea, I mean."

"You can help me, Amelia. I thank you. But first, will you not introduce your friend?"

Amelia's blush deepened. "This is Bianca della Tomelloso. She lives here, too."

The woman had the carriage of a queen and scornful dark eyes that appeared to find Dorothea wanting. She lifted her chin and said nothing.

Dorothea was not sure of the etiquette for meeting a mistress. It had never been covered by her finishing governess. She held out her hand. "You are Major Cassiday's woman. I am pleased to meet you."

S ix of Fox's exploring officers had been over the border, working in pairs, scouting the route that the part of the army that included Lion's squadron would take when Wellington gave the order to move into Spain.

Each pair in turn reported, using maps and sketches to explain places where the landscape might cause problems for the invasion, where an ambush might be devastating, where the army might camp with reasonable safety, and a dozen other details to support a successful crossing.

It took hours, and all the time, Lion wished he had been able to accept the clear invitation in Dorothea's eyes. He had to draw on a lifetime of discipline to attend to the briefing, and even then, his attention kept wandering to his wife, the sweet welcome he had enjoyed to the full last night, and his plans for the night to come.

When he came out of the command tent, though, Blythe was waiting with a grin. "Lady Harcourt is already at the mess tent, colonel."

Lion must have looked bewildered.

"For the party," Blythe explained. "The one to celebrate your marriage."

Lion managed to stifle his groan. "Good man, Blythe," he said. "You have it all set up?"

Blythe nodded, and began to explain the arrangements. Lion was relieved when they were interrupted by one of the exploring officers. "Come on," said Bear. "I would like the honour of being introduced to your wife."

Good idea. Dorothea must be wondering what was keeping him. He hoped she would not be overwhelmed by his men, who could be boisterous in their celebrations. He would rescue her, and show her that he meant to protect her, always.

But far from needing his protection, Dorothea was enthroned at one end of the mess tent, with Amelia on one side of her and Bianca on the other, while his officers had formed into lines to be presented to their colonel's lady.

Blythe had managed some welcome banners, put together a table laden with the snacks the Portuguese called petiscos, and rounded up some soldiers with musical instruments to play for dancing. Lion would have to remember to praise him.

Dorothea waved gaily when she saw Lion. She did not appear as if she had missed him. He gave himself a mental kick. What was he? Jealous? Just because a couple of dozen officers were slavering over his wife? Possessive was the word. He didn't mind admitting to being possessive, and who wouldn't be?

Jealousy was for lesser men, who were not married to the beautiful woman who had abandoned her courtiers and was coming towards him with a welcoming smile. "Lion! Your officers have been so kind, but I am glad you are here. They all want to dance with me and I told them I will not dance with anyone but you. Tell them, Lion."

"Not fair, Colonel," said one of the captains. "You and the majors have all the best ladies."

"Privileges of rank, captain," Lion told him. "Dorothea, whom haven't you met?"

The exploring officers all clamoured to be introduced, and it was during this that the Conde de Estombar arrived with Roderick Westinghouse. *What was Westinghouse doing here?* Lion supposed he could not follow his first impulse and throw the man out. Not when he was with a nobreza.

Westinghouse hovered on the edge of the group around Lion's wife, waiting for his chance to talk to Dorothea. Lion didn't mean to give it to him, but Dorothea said, "Let me find out what the horrid man wants.

Lion did not retreat far, though. He heard Westinghouse say, "Your father asked me to come to make sure you are being treated well."

"Exceedingly well," she replied, dignified as a queen. An ice queen, for every syllable dripped frost. "You may return to England and report to him, if indeed he sent you, that I am well and happy. Now, you will excuse me, Mr Westinghouse. I wish to spend some time getting to know my husband's officers."

She turned her back on the man in a comprehensive snub, and Lion glared the fool down when he would have stepped after her.

After that, they stayed long enough for Dorothea to meet every officer, and for Lion and Dorothea to have a single dance together, during which she whispered to him, "I am tired, Lion. May we not go home?" She licked her lips. "To that big bed?"

Lion could barely finish the dance, and was escorting Dorothea from the floor even as the last notes were playing. He checked in his headlong rush as they reached the opening to the tent, and coaxed Dorothea sideways to avoid Westinghouse, who lounged there, obviously drunk.

Lion resisted the urge to punch the man. It would offend the nobreza, and in turn, Lion's general. In any case, he had better things to do. He put his arm around Dorothea and hugged her close to his side as he hurried past the obnoxious man and into the dark.

A knock on his door woke him. "Lion!" It was Fox. "Lion, I'm sorry to disturb you, but you're needed."

Dorothea shifted in his arms. In the light of the candle they had left burning when they came together in the bed, he could see her eyes were open.

Fox rattled the door, but Lion had locked it. "Lion?" he called again.

"Can't it wait till morning?" Lion demanded. Dorothea's lips were so close he could not resist kissing them.

Fox sounded irritated. "No, Colonel. It cannot. Come on out, Lion. I don't want to shout about this."

Lion sighed. "Give me a minute," he shouted back.

Fox muttered from the other side of the door, but Lion couldn't make out the words.

He kissed his wife again. "I'm sorry, my love," he apologised in a whisper.

"Go and do your duty, husband," Dorothea replied. "I will be here when you return."

He put one hand on her bare flanks. "I will lock the door when I leave. You go to sleep. I don't know how long it will be."

She slipped out of bed, and walked around the room naked, picking up the clothing he had tossed aside in his haste to join with her, and bringing them to him in order—the shirt, the breeches, the stockings. She knelt to help him put those on. *A fetching view.* He didn't say it out loud, for he did not want to make her self-conscious. Though perhaps he should discourage her, for he was becoming aroused again.

She handed him his boots and went to fetch his waistcoat and uniform jacket, which were hanging over the back of a chair. In slightly more than the minute he had requested, he was dressed.

"Back to bed, my love. I don't want you to be in view when I open the door," he said. She gave a startled yelp and leapt for the bed, burrowing down into the blankets, and Lion heaved another sigh, wishing he could ignore whatever crisis two of the best majors in the British army could not deal with on their own. He would give anything except his honour and his duty to his men to follow his wife back into their bed and ignore the world.

One of the two best majors in the British army *was* the crisis.

Lion had never seen Michael Cassiday so drunk. Furthermore, the man famous throughout the regiment for his equitable temper was in a blind rage, even now needing to be restrained so that he didn't try to finish what he had started.

"Westinghouse made an unfortunate remark about Bianca," Fox explained. "I know that's not an excuse for attacking the man without warning, but you cannot blame a man for defending the reputation of his woman. Even if she is just a mistress."

Lion could blame him for mauling the civilian in front of a tent full of junior officers and causing an international incident into the bargain. The Portugese nobreza was beside himself with rage.

"To attack a guest of mine. It is an insult. I will have satisfaction, colonel."

It took Lion all too long to sort it all out. The surgeon first. He prescribed bed for Michael. Lion had the major dragged to a tent to sleep off his inebriation, with two guards posted to keep him there. Westinghouse was dazed, but more with the local port than with the beating he had taken, though his nose was broken and he'd have two black eyes by morning.

The Conde de Estombar took more effort. Lion apologised and promised retribution for the insult, which according to the nobreza, was felt by the entire Portuguese nobility. Fox exercised all of his charm, and Lion pointed out Westinghouse's offensive remarks about Michael's mistress (at which the nobreza sneered) and Lion's wife, which he took more seriously once Lion invoked the Harcourt and Ruthford titles.

Fortunately, the man was fluent in English, accented but intelligible, so Lion did not have to make his apologies, explanations, and promises in his own halting Portuguese or his slightly better Spanish. In the end, the conde loftily agreed to leave the matter to the British army, loaded Westinghouse into his carriage and left.

"That's it," Lion said. "I'm for bed. I'll deal with Cassiday when he is sober."

"What do you plan to do?" Fox asked. "I wouldn't like to see Michael broken to captain, but such a loss of control... Obviously he cannot stay in charge of the squadron."

Lion didn't want to think about it again tonight. He wanted his wife. He wanted to go to sleep and wake up to find that none of this had happened. He certainly was not going to make any decisions without further information.

"You could be right," he told Fox. "We'll see."

CHAPTER 12

Dorothea was clearly going to have to get used to Lion going away at a moment's notice. The meeting with his exploring officers as soon as they arrived back in camp, the interruption in the night to deal with a drunken brawl, and with breakfast, a message from Wellington, asking for Lion's presence at headquarters immediately.

"Of course, I do not mind," she replied mendaciously to his worried enquiry. "I knew you had to lead your part of the army. I will be here when you have time for me, and find things to do when you do not. You need not worry about me, Lion. I married an officer with responsibilities, and I do not mean to be a burden to you."

Which was all very well, but now he had ridden out of camp, with Bear, Fox and a platoon of troopers, she had no idea what to do with herself. Both Emily and Amelia viewed officers' wives as useless ornamentation, and Dorothea had no intention of being that.

But wait. How was this different to what I am trained for? Manage the house and its servants. Ensure that meals palatable to her husband were put on the table in a timely fashion. Look after the welfare of those who answered to her husband as servants or tenants, and more widely the welfare of the poor of the parish.

If she had married in England, she would not have hesitated to call the cook and the housekeeper to her and learn all about the house, and to question them and the local vicar about the estate and the surrounding area.

Who would be the equivalent in her current situation? Major Cassiday, perhaps. He was in disgrace after getting into a fight with Roderick Westinghouse, and had been left behind. He might be able to advise her. She wondered if the troops had a chaplain. He, too, could be helpful.

She would start, however, with Michael's mistress, if only because she shared a house with the woman. Bianca was a little stand-offish. Asking for her help and advice might attract scorn. On the other hand, she might appreciate it. It might break the ice between them.

Certainly, making friends with Bianca and asking her advice was a better idea than sitting here on the bench outside the farmhouse, staring at the road down which Lion had disappeared, and feeling sorry for herself.

She could also ask both women for information about other women who lived in the camp, and perhaps for some introductions. After all, even if neither of them had any more idea than Dorothea about the duties the colonel's wife might take to herself, they must at least know more than Dorothea did about the actual people.

Amelia was in the big living room, cutting up meat and vegetables at the kitchen table. Dorothea fetched a knife for herself and began chopping small yellow onions in half and stripping off the brown outer layers.

"You don't have to do that," Amelia objected. "A lady like you."

"Do we have a cook?" Dorothea asked.

"Just me," said Amelia. "One of the women from the camp comes in to clean, though, and she scrubs the pots."

"Well then," Dorothea said. "I want to eat and I want Lion to eat, so I will help to cook. Besides, it is more fun with two."

Amelia smiled, a quick shy glance and a curve of her lips that remained even after she looked back at her work. "It is," she confessed. "Bianca…" She flushed, and pressed her lips together, then said, "Michael is not well today. He spent the night… elsewhere. Bianca has gone to look after him."

"He drank too much last night, my husband said," Dorothea commented.

Amelia frowned. "It is not like him. And it is not like the Colonel to be so angry. Fox is worried about Michael. Lion has threatened to strip him of command; to demote him. But Dorothea, it was just one slip. It is not as if Michael makes a habit of getting drunk."

Dorothea frowned. Lion had seemed to her more concerned than angry, but she would not say that to Amelia. To discuss her husband's military decisions with his men or their wives seemed a sort of a betrayal. "We will have to see what happens when he returns," she said, vaguely.

Amelia took the hint. "What are your plans for the rest of the day, my lady?" At Dorothea's sharp look, she changed that to, "Dorothea, I mean."

"Actually, Amelia, I want your help. As I have told you, I do not wish to be a burden to my husband—just a piece of luggage that he drags behind him in the baggage train. But I have much to learn about the people and their lives before I can be of any real use. I have many questions. Can you answer them, or tell me who can?"

⁂

Lion was gone for five days. Michael Cassiday had been released late on the first day, sheepish and somewhat bewildered. He remembered little from the evening before, and did not know what had caused the fight with Roderick.

Bianca veiled her eyes, her proud face stiff with the effort to show no emotion. *She knows something.* Dorothea suppressed her questions. Bianca did not trust her, and would tell her nothing.

Instead, Dorothea. explained what she had done during the day and why. Amelia had introduced her to the chaplain, the surgeon, those officers she had not met the night before, and some of the senior civilians in the regiment's supply train. "A good start," she said, "but I really want to get to know the women."

Bianca looked up at that. "For why?" she demanded.

Dorothea was surprised at the question. "It is what wives of leaders do," she explained. Perhaps it was different in Portugal. "Our husbands manage their businesses or their estates or their troops. We wives make sure that the little things, the domestic dramas and tragedies, do not disrupt their plans. The women are our domain—they know what their men face, what they suffer, what they need. By talking to the women, we can discover the troubles that will become problems if they are allowed to grow."

Bianca nodded, a touch of approval softening the disdain she had shown since Dorothea arrived. "So it is in my country," she said. "Very well, Mrs O'Toole. I will translate."

She was as good as her word. Over the next few days, Dorothea met every woman and child in the supply train and their men. She also enlisted Blythe to introduce her to the enlisted men. Fortunately, she was good at remembering names, but even so, her head spun by the end of each day. It helped that her husband's people soon realised that Mrs O'Toole was prepared to listen to them. Their stories helped her to connect names to faces, as she remembered how they had come to be here, or what had happened to them, and the troubles they faced.

She began to pick up a word or two of Portuguese. Spanish, too, for many of the camp followers had come from Spain when the army returned to winter quarters.

"She called you 'Doña'," she said to Bianca one day, as they walked away from the tent that a sergeant in the regiment shared with his common-law wife. "Many of them do. In Spanish, it means 'my lady', does it not?"

Bianca shrugged. "More or less. You are my lady. I am my lady. In the army, it means little."

She did not appreciate Dorothea's curiosity. Dorothea almost took the hint, but she had been wondering for days, and it was, after all, her responsibility to smooth any difficulties that might become problems for Lion.

"Lion said Michael should marry you," she said, "and from what I have seen, he dearly loves you. What seems to be the problem?"

Bianca began to stiffen again, but then she laughed. "You are a determined woman, Mrs O'Toole." Dorothea had repeatedly asked her to call her by her given name, but Bianca had continued to maintain a formal distance, though at least she remember not to say Lady Harcourt.

Dorothea's commitment to the camp followers, or perhaps her persistence, had brought about a thaw, for Bianca said, "Very well, I shall tell you my whole sad story. Come. I shall make us both a chocolate, and I shall narrate the pitiful tale."

Back at the house, it was just the two of them. Amelia, who was much in demand for treating minor injuries and as a midwife, was away seeing an expectant mother on the other side of the camp, Blythe and Fox had gone with Lion, and Michael was, or so Bianca said caustically, working three times as hard as usual as if to make up for his trespasses.

She fetched a box from her room, and put it on the table, swung one of the kettles onto the fire, and came back to the table with a shallow bowl, a ladle, and two mugs. "Very well. Where to start?" She removed a grater and a tin from the box. "Michael buys this for me already made up," she said, removing a bar from the tin. "It is a mix of ground cacoa, honey and spices."

She began to grate the bar. "You are correct. I was born into a good family and gently raised. If you would be so good, Dorothea, please say nothing until I have finished. I have never told this story to anyone but Michael, my father, and my confessor."

Dorothea nodded her agreement.

Bianca began, "I was on my way from the convent where I was being schooled to my home when the French attacked me and my escort."

Her busy hands paused and she looked up, her proud face

suddenly bleak. "They killed the men who guarded me. I pray every day for the soul of my maid. The officer gave her to their men. I will not speak of what those soldiers did, or of what the officer did to me. I survived, and in the night, when they were all drunk, I escaped. I ran into Michael and his men. I showed them the French camp."

She returned to her grating, a fierce glow in her eyes. The smile that curved her lips was triumphant rather than amused. "They all died. The English had seen the condition I was in, and those evil pigs had left Maria where she lay. Fetch the water, please, Dorothea."

Dorothea, unable to think of anything to say in the face of Bianca's pride, found a heavy cloth for the hot handle and brought the kettle to the table.

"Michael took me home to my father, but when he heard what had happened, my father turned me away. He sent me back to the convent with a bride price, for he said that only the Lord Jesus would have me now. Instead, I stayed with Michael."

She scooped grated chocolate into each mug then carefully ladled boiling water on top. As she stirred, she continued. "That is the whole of it. I love Michael with all my heart, but it is difficult. There are so many reasons against our marriage. I am a ruined woman in the eyes of my people and his. Not just because of those French monsters, but because I have been his mistress. Major Foxton tells me that a man who marries his mistress will never be promoted in your English army, and I cannot stand in Michael's way."

Fox again. Dorothea was becoming a little annoyed with how free he was with his opinions. "I would not take Major Foxton as an expert on such a matter, Bianca," she said. "There are narrow-minded people in England, as well as Spain. But my husband says that marriage covers a multitude of sins."

Bianca continued stirring the drinks. "There is more. We are of two different faiths. Michael has explained it to me that he must belong to your English church, or he cannot be an officer in your army or work for your government. I would never let him give up his future so that we could marry."

Dorothea didn't understand. "But can he not go on being Church of England if you marry?"

Bianca shrugged. "A son or daughter of the true church cannot marry a heretic. The priests will not allow it. I mean no offence, my friend, but you English, most of you, do not follow the true faith. If I could find a priest prepared to perform the ceremony, you English would not recognise our marriage. And if we are married according to the English rite, my own church will consider us unwed."

She handed Dorothea a cup and took a sip from her own. "I cannot give up my church for Michael nor he for me. Only marriages in my church are real to my people, and only marriages in yours are real to yours. So, what difference?" The wry twist of her lips belied the sadness in her eyes. "I remain Michael's whore in the eyes of either his people or mine."

To Dorothea, the answer seemed obvious. "Then marry in both. Find a priest who will marry you to Michael in your own faith, and arrange for the chaplain to marry you in Michael's."

Dorothea sipped from the chocolate and closed her eyes to savour the flavour. When she opened them, the other woman was staring at her, eyes wide, a slight smile beginning.

"Two weddings? Is that legal?" she asked.

Dorothea had no intention of discussing her own two weddings. "I do not see how either church can object. If they do not recognise marriages by the other church, then you are not having two weddings."

"Hah!" said Bianca. "I like the way you think. Very well, Dorothea. I shall talk to Michael and we shall see."

Before they could speak further, Fox arrived. Lion had sent him back once before with messages and instructions, plus a letter for Dorothea. She hoped that this time Lion had come as well, but when she looked eagerly towards the door by which Fox had entered, he bowed with his usual charm.

"Dorothea, you are as lovely as ever. I am sorry to have to tell you that your husband is still with Wellington and the other generals. Alas, I too must return soon. Bianca, my love, when are you going to abandon Michael and run off with me?"

As he made the remark, Michael entered the building. *Did Fox seen him coming?* Dorothea shook off the thought. Fox was just joking of course, but it was a joke in poor taste.

Bianca, who had been relaxed and smiling, turned cold and haughty again, lifting her chin and looking down her nose at Fox. "Never, Major Foxton."

"Be careful, Fox," Michael said. "You'll not be insulting my Bianca, now."

Fox laughed. "Of course not, Cassiday. After what happened to Westinghouse? I would not dare." He performed a bow so low it was a mockery. "My humblest apologies, Doña Bianca. I did not mean to offend. It was merely a joke. I did not realise how sensitive a subject it would be."

His laughing eyes invited Dorothea to find Michael's reaction funny.

Dorothea was annoyed he had spoiled Bianca's good mood. "Such jokes are not pleasant for any but the jokester."

She read surprise and anger in Fox's expression before he covered it with another smile. "The Colonel's wife has spoken," he said. "Lady Harcourt, ma'am, I came to give you another note from your husband. Cassiday, I have more instructions from his lordship for you, too, and then I need to meet with my officers." He pulled a letter and a package from the satchel he carried, handing the letter to Dorothea and the package to Michael. He clicked his heels together and inclined his head. "If you will excuse me, Lion wants me back today."

Dorothea was even more irritated with Fox when she found he'd spent an hour in the camp and only saw Amelia by chance as he was leaving. Amelia was bubbling with delight that her husband had spent five minutes with her. Five minutes in which he had given her some mending to do and scolded her for not being at home when he got there.

"He said I should ask you to talk Lion into forgiving Major Cassiday, Dorothea. But I said I did not need to, for you and Major Cassiday have become friends. He was pleased, for Major Cassiday is his friend, too."

Fox had an odd idea of how to be a friend. Dorothea did not share her thoughts with Amelia, though. Let the poor woman stay happy. As for Dorothea, she had a note from Lion, assuring her of his love and telling her he would be back the following day. She went to sleep with the note under her pillow and Lion's handkerchief tucked into her night rail, next to her skin.

CHAPTER 13

Lion and Fox rode ahead of the column of troopers, driven mostly by Lion's eagerness to return to Dorothea. According to Fox, Dorothea had been keeping herself busy in his absence. Fox was inclined to be annoyed that she had employed a couple of the camp followers to cook for them and do their laundry. Lion wished he had thought of it. Amelia was wife to a major now, and should not still be doing the work of a servant.

"She has been wandering all over the camp, making a nuisance of herself with the families," Fox told him. "You'll have to have a word with her, Lion."

Lion would reserve judgement until he had talked to his wife. *Which would be within the hour, for that odd shaped rock ahead marked the turn to their camp.*

He resisted the urge to spur his horse on. It was too early. "I'll talk to her," he told Fox. *And listen, too.* Fox had an odd kick in his gallop when it came to socialising between the classes.

Fox fell silent for a while, and they'd passed Almeida and had the camp within sight when he rode up beside Lion again. "Dorothea and Cassiday have been getting on well," he commented. "Nothing for you to worry about, Lion, I'm sure. Even if she has spent more time with our good major than she has with you."

Lion repressed a sigh. Fox had been making remarks like this ever since he arrived back in Portugal. It was just Fox's way, but Lion was finding it annoying. "I know I have nothing to worry about," Lion told him. "My wife loves me, and I trust her."

"Oh, good," Fox said. "I am sure you are right to do so."

Lion shook off a slight disquiet to wave to the camp's sentries, who had been watching them approach. "Welcome back, Colonel," said one of them.

"Thank you," Lion said. "Glad to see you're alert."

"Always, sir," the other man assured him. "Are we on the move, then?"

"Soon, trooper," Lion assured him. "Soon."

Within a week, or so Wellington intended. They were ready, rested, and well supplied. "Next year," he predicted, "our winter quarters will be in Spain, or even France!"

Both soldiers grinned at that. "France, I say, sir," the first one said.

Lion returned the grin and sent his horse forward again. The farmhouse was just behind the second line of sentries, on the edge of the camp. Lion dismounted outside and tossed his reins to Blythe, who had been trailing Lion and Fox, and had caught up when the two men paused to talk to the sentries.

Fox was close behind him as he opened the door, walking in to hear Michael say, "I hope you can persuade Lion to forgive me, Dorothea. I still don't remember what happened, but I know I should have handled it better."

It was the three of them: Dorothea, Michael and Amelia. *At least she is not alone with Michael*, Lion thought, and then was ashamed he had let Fox's nonsense influence him.

Amelia saw them first and stood, with an exclamation of delight. "Major Foxton! And Colonel O'Toole, too. Dorothea, your husband is here."

Dorothea already knew. She had turned towards him, beaming, her hands held out. He took them and pulled her towards him, kissing her in a passionate claiming that was, he acknowledged in his innermost heart, at least in part a demonstration—telling Michael and anyone else who needed to know that Dorothea was his. *You are being ridiculous, Lion. The woman loves you.*

Perhaps when he had her in his arms, joined to her in the most intimate of ways, his disquiet would settle. "Come," he said. He led her to their bedchamber and shut the door.

"I need you, wife." That was all the warning he gave her as he pressed her up against the door, his mouth devouring hers, his hands reaching buttons and ties until he had her bare to the waist and his mouth was drawing moans from her.

"But Lion, everyone will know what we are doing," she objected, but his hand, drawing up her skirts and seeking her heat, knew her body was responding to his as she thrust against his seeking hand. Still, he withdrew his mouth for long enough to reassure her. "None of them will say a word, my love. You are my wife and I have missed you. Have you missed me?"

"So much," she assured him, and whimpered as he reached into her core with a second finger.

"Then take off your clothes, Dorothea, and show me how much." He was done with words. He took his hands from her long enough to pull the dress down, so that several buttons popped off and rolled across the room. Underneath, she was wearing light jumps that laced at the front.

He reached for the dagger in his boot and cut the laces. She shrugged out of it, her pupils dilated in passion, her breath coming in short pants.

"You too," she demanded.

"Next time." He shrugged out of his uniform jacket lest the braid and buttons abrade her tender skin. He undid his trouser flap. He had no time for anything more, for she had removed her chemise and he had to have her.

He picked her up, embracing her, and she pressed into his body, kissing him as if she wanted to climb inside him. Which was close to what he wanted, and he carried her to the bed and fell onto it, taking his weight on one elbow while his other hand guided his entry into her wet and welcoming warmth. It was a homecoming. This was where he belonged; perhaps the only place he had ever truly been at home since his mother died.

An unwanted thought surfaced. *If Dorothea ever betrays me, I will be destroyed.* He thrust it away as her body rose to meet his and they settled into the rhythm she had so quickly learned in their few days together.

Dear God, I love this woman.

She came, shrieking his name so loudly that half the camp must have known that their colonel had pleasured his woman. Her spasms drove him over the edge, and he emptied himself into her, on and on, until he collapsed on her. He retained just enough sense to twist slightly so that at least some of his weight was carried by the mattress.

As his senses returned, he realised that he'd just taken his wife in nothing but her stockings and shoes, while he was still all but fully dressed. He winced with shame. "My love, was I rough? I am so sorry. I should have been more patient. I should at least have taken my boots off!"

Dorothea sounded breathless. "Lion," she said. "It was thrilling."

"Next time," he promised, "I will thrill you with more finesse."

⁂

Lion walked out of his bedchamber at peace with the world. Dorothea was still asleep—*the sleep of the well-pleasured*, Lion thought as he closed the bedchamber door as quietly as he could. Amelia was already up, and was frying bacon and eggs on a skillet over embers in the hearth. Blythe must have given her the provender he had brought from headquarters.

"Coffee, Colonel?" she asked. "I am making breakfast for Major Foxton. Can I fetch you a plate?"

Lion was suddenly remarkably hungry, which was unsurprising given how physically active he had been in the night. "Yes, thank you. Breakfast would be very welcome. I can pour my own coffee, Mrs Foxton."

He carried his mug out into the morning sun, where Fox was already sitting on the bench under the front window.

"I didn't expect to see you up so early," Fox commented. "Busy night, wasn't it?"

Lion bristled. Admittedly, he and Dorothea had not been quiet, but the comment was in poor taste.

Fox didn't seem to notice. "I am glad you have some compensations for your hasty marriage," he commented.

That was an odd thing to say. "I have Dorothea," Lion pointed out.

Fox chuckled. "Yes, I heard."

Lion glared at him. "Enough of that, Fox. Show my wife some respect."

"Sorry, Lion. It's just, it seems so unfair you didn't know you were earl-in-waiting until after you'd taken a merchant's daughter to wife. There are better-born women—ladies—with dowries her equal or better, and you could have had your pick. I blame our grandfather."

"Don't say that Fox. Don't even think it. I count myself the luckiest man alive that I was there to rescue her from Westinghouse. I love her, Fox, and she loves me." He smiled out over the camp, recovering some of the peace with which he'd started the day.

He wanted his cousin to understand. "You can't know what it is like. My life has been turmoil and chaos since my mother died, but Dorothea makes sense of everything. She is my order and my peace. Be glad for me, cousin."

Fox looked blank for a moment, as if he could not understand Lion's words. Then he lifted his cup to sip his coffee and looked away, across the sea of tents where earlier risers than they were already busy. "That's good then," he said.

She loves me, Lion reminded himself again. And then, unbidden, *And I do love her. If ever I do not, chaos is come again.*

"What was that, Lion?" Fox asked.

Did I say that out loud? He must have. "Nothing," he told his cousin. "Look, here is your wife with our breakfast."

Dorothea had been busy while Lion was away. The first sign of her activities was the woman who appeared half way through the afternoon, shortly after he and Dorothea emerged from their bedchamber. She was there, apparently, to prepare the dinner. Fox was inclined to be indignant that Dorothea had taken the job away from Amelia.

"You were not to know, Dorothea," he said, his tone patronising. "It is the job of a soldier's wife to put food on the table, and it is the one thing Amelia does well."

Amelia hunched her shoulders. "I am sorry, Major Foxton," she said.

"You *are* doing your job, Amelia," Dorothea told her. "Fox, it is the job of an officer's wife, as it is the task of the wife of any gentleman, to put food on the table by supervising those who acquire it, those who prepare it, and those who clean up after it. Just as it is the job of an officer to survey the terrain by sending out exploring officers."

"A hit," Michael Cassiday quoted. "A veritable hit."

Fox went white around the nostrils, a sure sign he was about to lose his temper. Lion moved up beside Dorothea and frowned a warning at his cousin, and Fox thought better of whatever he had been about to say.

"You make a good point, my wife," Lion said. "What else have you been up to while I was away?"

"Dorothea and the other two ladies have been visiting around the camp, Lion, to see where they can give advice and practical help," Michael said. His smile at Dorothea was a little warm for Lion's liking.

He went on to explain, "For example, the women Amelia and Dorothea chose to come and cook? All of them have small children to feed and need to take in extra work to make ends meet, especially when their men's pay is late arriving. Dorothea suggested we hire a different one for each day. The women themselves have made up a roster and those who are not working take it in turns to care for the children of those who are. All of them get a little bit of money and the help of the others."

"The same with our laundry," Dorothea added. "It assists the families and I thought if the wives were happier, the soldiers would be less worried about them and more content. I am sorry if you object, Lion. I thought to make your burden easier."

Why would Lion object? "It is marvellous," he said. "Thank you for thinking of it, Dorothea."

"Actually, Michael," Dorothea corrected, "splitting up the jobs between a number of the women who most needed the work was Bianca's idea, though I was the one who suggested they organise themselves and share the care of the children."

Dorothea had got Bianca to take an interest in the camp followers? The same Bianca who had refused since Michael brought her home to do anything except a bit of mending for Michael? The Bianca who was, now he came to think about it, humming over her sewing for the first time ever in his hearing? Lion's wife was a walking miracle. "Well done," he said, approvingly. "I look forward to hearing about your other improvements."

A knock on the door interrupted them at that moment. With an internal sigh, Lion got up to fetch his coat and hat for whatever crisis had arisen that needed his attention. Instead, the corporal who entered at Michael's barked command faced Dorothea instead.

"My lady," he said. "Mrs O'Toole, ma'am, Mrs Fraser wants you to come. It's her Joey, ma'am."

Dorothea caught up her shawl. "What has happened to young Joseph?" she asked.

The corporal cast a worried glance at Michael and then at Lion.

"It is Hector, isn't it," Dorothea concluded. "Lion, I need you. What Corporal Kelly doesn't want to say is that Hector Fraser is drunk again, and threatening to beat his wife's son. Or beating him?"

"Beating his wife," the corporal said. "The little boy is hiding."

"Dorothea," Lion objected, "unless the man is on duty, having a bit too much to drink is not a disciplinary matter, or I'd have every man in every troop up on charges all the time. And a man has a right to discipline his son. And his wife."

"Young Joseph is four, Lion," Dorothea retorted, "and the last time Fraser was drunk, he knocked his wife unconscious for smiling and broke the little boy's arm for the gross infraction of existing."

Bianca had put down her sewing and was wrapping herself in her shawl. "I'll come with you, Dorothea. Lord Harcourt, Fraser took in another man's woman when her husband was killed. He promised to treat the baby as his own, but he lied. He ignores the boy when sober, but when he is drunk, he tries to kill the poor ninito."

Dorothea was already halfway to the door. Lion and Michael exchanged glances. Both fetched their coats and followed after their ladies.

"She is a lioness, your wife," Michael said with admiration as they walked home after handing Fraser over to be locked up until he was conscious and sober. Dorothea and Bianca had taken Mrs Fraser to the surgeon to have her bruises salved and her dislocated shoulder put back into place. Fraser had been dragging the poor woman by one arm across the camp, yelling for Joey to come out and be shot, when Dorothea and Bianca had confronted him.

"Private Fraser," Dorothea had demanded. "Let go of your wife."

Fraser was so surprised he did as he was told. Then, as Bianca whisked Mrs Fraser away, he realised what he'd done and roared. "You Spanish bitch! Let go of my whore!" He took a step towards Bianca. Michael punched him in the belly then thumped him on the back of the neck as he fell.

Little Joey had crawled from hiding and run to his mother as soon as Fraser was on the ground. Little was right. If Lion had not been told the boy's age, he'd have picked him as being two years at the most—a half-starved little mite with his mother's large brown eyes. He had shrunk away from Lion—or, more probably, Lion's uniform—but had allowed Corporal Kelly to carry him to the surgeon's tent.

"Perhaps now Mrs Fraser will consider another suitor," Michael commented. "Bianca says she has been afraid another man might also resent her son, but Dorothea has offered to interview candidates to help her find one who will be kind. Mrs Fraser is a good cook, apparently, so there will be no shortage of men eager to have her."

"Fraser never married her?" Lion asked. The solution sounded like a good one, but a legal marriage would make it awkward.

Michael shook his head. "Another stubborn Spanish woman who won't marry outside of her own kind," he grumbled. "Though probably Fraser never offered."

Which reminded Lion of something Bear had told him while they were in Freinada. "Why didn't you tell me Westinghouse assaulted Bianca?" he asked.

Michael shrugged. "You were gone by the time I sobered up, Lion, I'm ashamed to say. Besides, I had no idea until Bianca told me. Apparently, when I found him, he had her pinned down on the ground and was trying to open the buttons of his pants' flap without taking his hand off her mouth. And I don't see that it makes a difference. He was a civilian and a guest. I should have dragged him out the front and had him thrown out. Instead, I gather that I tried to kill him. Your wife told you, I suppose?"

So Dorothea knew? Perhaps Bianca told her. Or was she so much in Michael's confidence that he had?

"Bear told me. Dorothea thinks I should reinstate you, but I told her I didn't demote you. It's not like you to drink so much you don't know what you are doing, Michael. I don't expect it to happen again. After the way you and Bianca met, I don't blame you for losing your mind. And Westinghouse is a pig. Besides, I need every officer I have for the drive into Spain."

CHAPTER 14

Dorothea could not imagine being happier. Lion said he was proud of her. He thanked her for her work among the woman. "It is my job, Lion," she explained. "As your wife, the wives and families of your men are my responsibility."

"It is part of your job," Lion said, gently scolding, but with a broad smile that showed a playful side to him she had not seen before. "Take off your clothes, my wife, for another part of your job is even more important."

She blushed as she told him that what he had in mind was not a job, but a joy, and he laughed and popped off another set of buttons in his haste to take her to bed again. Though a bed was not actually involved this time. She foresaw quite a bit of mending in her future, and every stitch worth it.

She was less happy when he rode out with Captain Gavenor—who was called Bear and looked like one—and two of the other exploring officers the following day. That was part of her job, too. Waving goodbye with a smile and welcoming him back without complaint or recrimination.

She had her own work to do, even though she missed Lion every moment, as if she had a hole in her heart that only his presence could fill.

She, Amelia and Bianca, who had proved to be able lieutenants, were busy every day, meeting with the women amongst the camp followers—the wives, mistresses, prostitutes and tradeswomen who travelled with the army's baggage train and performed a variety of essential services that kept the army functioning.

Indeed, most regiments recognised how essential they were in the policy that provided transport for one wife, chosen by ballot, for every ten soldiers (or a different number, depending on the regiment). They cooked. They scavenged or bargained for food and other supplies. They cleaned, washed laundry, and mended. They treated minor wounds and nursed the sick. They collected firewood, and performed one hundred other services without which the army would falter and collapse.

Some of them were officially recognised with payment. Other services, including the comfort of their bodies, were ignored by officialdom and taken for granted by the men. If a woman was widowed, she had better find herself another husband or at least a protector immediately, for otherwise she would be expected to service a line of those who had no woman to meet their physical needs.

Dorothea, alive now to the demands of her own desire, wondered how women could do such intimate things with multiple men, especially men they barely knew. She was not surprised at the choice to select one from among the many made by those suddenly widowed. Widows such as the former Mrs Fraser, now Mrs Kelly. She was much happier, Corporal Kelly being a kindly man who had become little Joey's hero and demi-god.

Only two things disturbed Dorothea's satisfaction with life. Lion had returned only to leave again. And she had lost his mother's handkerchief. She had dropped it somewhere or—and she was loathe to believe this—one of her roster of daily cooks and maids had stolen it.

B ear had to be right that someone was leaking information to the enemy. One of Lion's officers or someone with access to his officers. Probably someone in the cadre of exploring officers known as the Zoo, for they had been the focus of most of the resulting attacks, or one of Lion's aides, which meant Michael, Fox, or their most senior captains. Or a person they trusted enough to talk to, which could mean one of the wives or mistresses, or a personal servant.

Bear and his colleagues had put into action the advice Bear had given to Lion—alternate plans they did not discuss with anyone else. On thirteen excursions into Spain to scout the paths, six had followed the official plan. Four of those had been interrupted by French patrols when none should be there. Of those that followed plans known only to Bear and the exploring officers involved, not one ran into trouble.

Just to be certain, Lion went out with Bear to meet an officer who had been living among the French in disguise. Chameleon, they called him, but he preferred to answer to the name Max. A completely different name appeared on his pay records. The first two were nicknames. Lion suspected the official name was likewise fictional.

The assigned place for the meeting was a cantina in a small mountain village near the border between Spain and Portugal. Bear and Lion arrived an hour earlier than the time Bear had shared with Lion and his senior officers, and settled at the top of a little ruined keep that overlooked the village.

Max joined them a good half hour before the meeting time, climbing to their level so silently he was seated beside them before they realised he had arrived. He handed a package to Bear, saying, "My report," in a voice that was not much more than an exhaled breath.

Bear opened it and passed it to Lion. It was, like all of Max's reports, succinct. He had spent four weeks in a French winter camp, undetected. He didn't specify, but Lion knew he would have passed from one identity to another, picking character types that most people ignored, never keeping an identity long enough to be noticed. Max was very good at all his varied, skills, including the one that had earned him the name Maximum Force.

"This is confirmation," Lion whispered to Bear. "Someone is reporting on us and our plans." He handed the report to Bear, who swiftly scanned it and cursed, long and low.

Max watched them, saying nothing.

Lion's mind was racing. They had to find the traitor. They had to assume that every preparation Lion had made for the invasion over the border into Spain was known to the enemy, and change what they were planning.

"What are the chances that they have a chameleon in our camp?" he asked. He was clutching at straws. If the information was not coming from a French spy with the same exceptional skills as Max, it was being sold by one of his own. Furthermore, at least one of the messages Max had managed to see referred to plans known only to his senior officers. So, one of them was either a traitor or had confided in one.

"Lion," Bear said, nodding at the village below.

Movements in the shadows resolved into soldiers in French uniforms, taking up hidden posts around the entrance to the cantina. "If further proof were needed…" he sighed.

"It cannot be the Greek witch and her uncle," Bear pointed out. "They are nine months gone." Yannas and Elektra Nomikos had escaped hanging by going over to the French, or so Lion assumed. They had disappeared into the night and hadn't been heard of since. The woman had been lover to one of Lion's exploring officers, and had left him with a broken heart. After her disappearance the poor man had found out she'd had other lovers as well, which nearly destroyed him. Women could be the devil.

"If there is a chameleon in the camp, I can find him or her," Max offered. "Like knows like."

"As for the officers," Lion decided, "I have an idea. An urgent change of plans that will be, instead, a trap for the traitor."

L ion had not, of course, told Fox or Cassiday where he was going or why. They knew only that he had ridden off with Bear and stayed away overnight. He had to suspect everyone, though not his wife, of course. She didn't have it in her. And even if she did, the leaks had started long before he even met her, and certainly before she joined him in Portugal.

He didn't let Dorothea know the purpose of his trip, though. He trusted her. Of course he did. Any doubts he had were unfounded; he knew that. It was just it was army business, and nothing to do with her. He was sorry he had to spend so much time away from her, but she knew when she married him that he was a serving officer, and she had promised not to interfere with his duty. She had no right to complain. Nor did she, to be fair.

He expected to find her waiting for him and was disappointed Fox was the only one at the farmhouse when he arrived. He was sitting at the table, drinking wine and tearing pieces from a bread roll with his teeth.

"Where is my wife?" Lion asked.

"Off in the camp somewhere with mine," Fox answered. "You can't expect her to sit around waiting for you to return, Lion. You've spent more time apart since your wedding than you've spent together. Why, Dorothea has lived with me and Cassiday longer than with you."

He took another bite and muttered, "And *I'm* not a threat to your marriage."

Lion decided not to take any notice. Fox thought Amelia should be dancing attendance on him every minute of every day, and had already given Lion his sour opinion of Dorothea's insistence on involving herself and Amelia in the lives of the camp followers.

"I'll send someone to tell her I am home," he said, refusing to let Fox know of his disappointment that Dorothea was not at home. He opened the door and stopped a passing soldier, gave him the message, and came back inside to help himself to a drink from the jug at Fox's elbow.

Fox shot him a glance and returned to brooding over his wine. Lion took a mouthful and grimaced. A bit sour for his taste. Probably a local pressing and sold while it was too new. Still, it would do to wash the bread down.

"I don't know how to tell you this, Lion," Fox said, "But I am your cousin and your oldest friend, and someone has to do it."

"Spit it out, then," Lion said. No one ever stopped Fox from saying what he had a mind to, and Lion just wanted to get it over with before Dorothea got back.

"Bianca has left," Fox said.

Lion hadn't expected that. "Left? You mean permanently?"

Fox nodded. "Had a huge fight with Cassiday and walked out." He took more wine in a gulp. "I couldn't help but hear what they said," he admitted. "That's how I found out."

Lion could not resist breaking the silence that followed. "What did you find out, Fox?"

"Bianca woke to hear Cassiday talking in his sleep. Lion, he was talking about becoming Dorothea's lover on the trip here. I swear I didn't know, though I realised they had become friends."

"It's nonsense," Lion said. "I don't believe a word of it."

"Cassiday admitted it," Fox insisted. "I couldn't believe it myself, until I heard it with my own ears."

Lion shook his head. "Then he lied."

Fox grimaced, pity in his eyes. "I know you want to believe that, Lion. Bianca left yesterday afternoon. Ask your wife whose bed she slept in last night. Ask her what has become of the handkerchief that you gave her."

Lion, who was staring furiously at the table, looked up at that. "My handkerchief."

"Cassiday has it in his pocket, Lion. I saw it."

Lion surged to his feet, ready to lay his cousin out on the floor for his lies, but before he could, Fox said, "There's more. She was meeting someone. I can't be certain of who the man was. I was too far away. But it was Dorothea, beyond a doubt. A short woman in an English walking gown? She was up in the edges of the fortifications around the village, where the passages into town give cover. I was coming back from…" he looked down at the table, veiling his eyes.

He had been visiting a lover, in other words. Lion didn't like his tom cat behaviour, but there was no point in objecting. Unless Fox had forced someone, which was directly against orders, and Fox was skilled at using charm rather than force.

Lion should stop him now. These accusations against his wife couldn't be true. But before he could force his tongue to unlock, Fox spoke again. "It looked to me like Westinghouse. I didn't see his face, but he was the right shape and size, and there was something about the way he carried himself…"

"If you plan to tell me that Dorothea is having an affair with Westinghouse, stubble it," Lion said, dryly.

"No. Not that," said Fox. "Any fool could see she doesn't like him, and there was no kiss or embrace or anything of that kind. Indeed, it looked to me like an argument. Perhaps she has already told you what it was about?"

Lion shook his head. Fox was talking nonsense. He was mistaken about what he saw, and whom.

Fox hadn't finished. "It crossed my mind… No. It is ridiculous."

"Go on," Lion commanded. "Don't stop now."

"I just thought that maybe it was all planned. Brabant sells cloth to the armies, right? He has got rich off the back of it. Richer, I suppose. I'm not suggesting he's a traitor, precisely, but if he wanted to slow the war down, it would have been a good tactic to drop his daughter in front of you. He pretended to be angry about the elopement, but you have to agree he came around quickly."

Fox poured himself another drink. "Westinghouse did not have two pennies to rub together, Lion. How could he afford a ship to Portugal? And what is he really doing here? I heard him myself, your first night back in camp, telling your wife he had been sent here by her father."

Fox shrugged. "Anyway. Think about it. I hope I am wrong."

So did Lion. Not about Westinghouse. He'd be happy to see the man hanged or shot. But Dorothea could not be part of it. Could she? He wanted to ignore Fox's accusations and insinuations. Fox meant well, but he did tend to see the worst in people. But Lion couldn't leave it at that. For the sake of his men. Hell, for his own sake and the sake of the future he dreamed of. He had to find out the truth behind what his cousin had told him.

Dorothea hurried back to the farmhouse, leaving Amelia behind to wash the new mother and her baby. Amelia had actually delivered the baby, but Dorothea was as proud as if she had done it herself. She was useful, in any case, even if all she had done was hold the mother's hand and tell her how well she was doing.

Lion had sent her a message well over an hour ago, but he would understand she could not have left just then. Not before the baby was born. Not when Amelia was depending on her to give the mother comfort and support.

She hurried into the farmhouse. No one was in the main room, but she could hear someone moving around the bedchamber she shared with Lion. Yes. There he was. For some reason, he was searching through her truck.

"Lion?" she said. "Can I help you to find something?"

"My mother's handkerchief, Dorothea," he said, something unsettling glittering in his eyes. "Can you find my mother's handkerchief for me?"

Oh dear. "I cannot," she admitted. "I am so sorry, Lion. I have been hunting for it everywhere. I keep it under my pillow at night and in a pocket under my gown during the day. But the night you got back from headquarters and we…" She blushed. "I didn't think of it when I went to bed." *Because I could not think of anything but you and what you were doing to me.* "I looked for it in the morning. My dress was there, but not my pocket. I have asked the laundresses, and search everywhere. I cannot think what has happened to it."

She reached out to touch Lion and he flinched away. "Are you saying it was stolen?" he demanded. "Is that your story? That you left my mother's handkerchief lying on the floor and someone crept into our bedchamber while we slept and stole it? But left everything else untouched?" His voice, rather than rising with rage, was lowering in volume until it was almost a whisper. Somehow, his quiet anger was far more frightening than her father's shouts.

She did her best to keep her composure. After all, her beloved husband, angry though he might be, would never hurt her. "I do not know, Lion. At first, I thought it must have been flung somewhere." She blushed again. "But I have hunted and hunted." She could feel tears rising and she forced them back. "It was your mother's, I know, and precious to you. Precious to me, too, because you trusted it to me, and I have let you down. I am so sorry."

He turned his back on her. "Your sorrow will not bring back what is lost."

"Lion?" she ventured. "Corporal Meadows' wife has had a little girl. Amelia says they are both well."

He faced her then, scowling, and she kept talking, not knowing what else to do. "That is why I did not come immediately when I received your message. She was about to give birth, and I needed to stay to help. You understand, Lion, don't you?"

Once again, she reached out to him, and once again, he evaded her touch.

"I have a report to write for Picton," he said, his voice cold. "I will be back later." He walked out the door without a further word.

Dorothea followed as far as the farmhouse door, and watched her husband stride across the camp. His steps were shorter and faster than usual, and his back was stiff. He was angry. She knew the handkerchief had meant a lot to him, but she hadn't thought he would be so upset. If only she had not lost it.

She did not hear Fox's approach until he spoke beside her. "Lion looks agitated about something."

"He is furious," Dorothea agreed. "I lost his mother's handkerchief, Fox. And I think he was also upset because I was not here when he arrived back."

Fox nodded. "It is disconcerting for a husband when his wife puts other people first. He begins to think she doesn't care about him."

His grim glare across the camp made Dorothea look in the same direction. Amelia was trudging back home, looking exhausted. "She has been up all night, Fox," Dorothea told him. "Mrs Meadows sent for us just after we had gone to bed. She had a hard time of it, poor woman, but—thanks to Amelia—the baby was safely born."

"She should have been at home," Fox growled. "With me."

Dorothea almost pointed out that he had gone out early in the evening, but perhaps he had come back later. Poor Fox, if he had been waiting for Amelia all night and most of the day. "Don't be hard on her," she begged. "She was only trying to help."

He chuckled and turned a laughing smile towards her. "What a dreadful opinion you must have of me, Dorothea. You and she have been out doing your charitable work. I am very happy, for the Meadows and their new baby, and for the other good the pair of you are doing. Don't worry about me and Amelia. And don't worry about Lion, either. I will have a word with him."

Dorothea watched while Fox greeted Amelia affectionately, asked after the baby, and told his wife to go to bed and sleep. "You look tired, Mrs Foxton."

"I have promised Mrs Meadows another blanket," Amelia said. "I will take it to her, and then sleep."

Fox gave her a pat on her shoulder. "You do that, my dear. Away with you."

To Dorothea, he said, "I'll go and talk to Lion now. All will work out exactly as it should, dear Dorothea."

How nice of Fox. Perhaps Dorothea had been too hasty in judging him.

It had been years since Lion's temper so overwhelmed him that he had to walk it off. That had been his Grandda O'Toole's advice, back when Lion was a mourning angry boy. "When the red rage comes, Lion, walk away. Give yourself time to get it under control."

To be obliged to walk away from Dorothea! Lion could hardly bear it. He strode around the camp, speaking to no one. By the time Fox found him, he had been able to assume at least a facade of calm. He would have to maintain it. It was the only way to find out whether Dorothea was a traitor to the King, or merely the domestic variety—a traitor to him. Or, a sliver of hope insisted, not a traitor at all.

It was hard to maintain his resolve when Fox told him that Dorothea had asked Fox to advocate for Michael Cassiday. "She wants him given back his command of the squadron," Fox said.

That was odd. Lion had never taken away Cassiday's command, though he had threatened to do so. Furthermore, he'd told Cassiday that he was forgiven, though he'd never actually mentioned it to Fox.

Lion shrugged off the discrepancy. Perhaps Cassiday didn't tell Dorothea that his command was safe because he felt uncomfortable discussing her husband with her.

And there was Cassiday, escorting a carriage towards the camp. "Here he comes," Fox said. "Come, Lion. Let's hide and watch how he greets Dorothea."

He led Lion to the back of the farmhouse. The window above the kitchen scullery bench allowed them a view of the interior of the building. A cloth blind filled the gap rather than glass, but they could see through the gaps around the edges, and they would invisible to those inside unless someone was right up by the window.

Dorothea was sitting at the table, drooping over a cup from which steam rose. She looked miserable. For a moment, Lion yearned to comfort her, but he stiffened his resolve. The whole point of this snooping around was to find out whether she was a lying jade.

The door swung open. The sun lit the back of the person who entered, casting his face into shade, but Lion knew him by his walk. Cassiday.

Another traitor, and so he proved to be, because he took two hasty steps forward and called out, "Dorothea! They agreed! One is done, and the other is set for this coming Wednesday, and we owe it…" his volume dropped to a normal conversational level, but Lion had heard enough.

Especially since Dorothea had held both hands out to Cassiday and he was swinging her around, both of them laughing.

Lion could feel his heart breaking. She did not love him. Perhaps she had never loved him. He had been so certain, but there she was, right in front of his eyes, celebrating with her lover.

Then, to Lion's surprise, Bianca, Cassiday's Spanish mistress, entered the room, and joined the happy laughing couple. Fox had said she had left Cassiday, so why did he put his arm around her? When Dorothea was standing right there? Bianca's own eyes shone, and she seemed to be celebrating as well. What on earth was going on?

Then Bianca took Lion's mother's handkerchief from her skirt and handed it to Cassiday. Dorothea spoke. "Lion's handkerchief!" Lion could hear that through the surging rage that consumed him, but nothing more. Their voice dropped low again.

The handkerchief once more changed hands, from Cassiday to Dorothea, and she held it to her cheek. The bitch. The faithless whore. To touch something that came from her lover so gently, with so much emotion. His mother's handkerchief! She had defiled it.

For that, and for all her treacheries, she must pay. But first, he had to regain control of himself, for if he stepped into the farmhouse now, he would kill them, Dorothea and Cassiday both. His deceivers. The people he had trusted above all others.

Fox said something Lion could not hear through the roaring anger that filled him. Lion shook his head and kept walking. Fox took his arm. Lion shook him off. Fox spoke again and Lion barked at him, "At ease, Major. Stay here, and leave me be."

Lion walked away.

He didn't get far before a voice penetrated his chaotic thoughts. A woman's voice, but not *hers*. "Colonel. Colonel. Is there something the matter?"

He stopped. It was Amelia. There was something he wanted to

ask Amelia. "Where were you last night," he demanded, his voice harsh.

She cringed away and her eyes darted in every direction, as if looking for escape. "With Mrs Meadows, Colonel. Helping her. She was having her baby."

"All night?" he demanded, annoyed at her tremulous voice. He wasn't going to hit the woman, for goodness sake.

"From when they called us in the late evening," she agreed.

"Us? Who was with you?" he demanded. Perhaps Dorothea had an alibi. Perhaps Fox was mistaken. But no. Amelia was looking guiltily around as if making up a reply. Whatever she said next would be an untruth.

She stumbled over the answer. "Your wife, sir. My lord. Dorothea. Lady Harcourt, I mean."

"You lie," he accused, and the colour drained from her face. "My wife was with her lover last night. I know this to be true."

Still, she stuck to her prevarications, faithful to her faithless mistress. "No, my lord. Lady Harcourt loves only you, my lord. She has no other lover. Your wife was with me. You can ask anyone. Ask Mrs Meadows. Ask Major Foxton."

Lion realised his fists were clenched. He had to walk away. Otherwise, he would break his solemn vow to never strike a woman, and Amelia was not the traitor. No. *That would be my jade of a wife.*

CHAPTER 15

There was no peace to be had in the camp. Everywhere, soldiers cared for their horses or their kit, amused themselves with cards or dice, whittled, played musical instruments, danced, told jokes and tall stories. Everywhere, soldiers' women bustled about with laundry or food, or chased after the children, or strolled with their husbands.

Lion turned away from one couple, gazing into one another's eyes under a tree, hand in hand. He walked out past the sentries. Inner ring of six. Ten paces on, an outer ring of eight. In the daylight, fourteen were enough to watch the entire perimeter, and at least five kept their eyes on him as he moved across the open ground beyond.

He skirted the hill that held the village. It and its fortifications dominated the surrounding area, and his officers had placed sentry posts on several of the arrowhead-shaped walls to give warning of any troops approaching. Today, he wasn't planning to visit any of them. Instead, he kept walking until he reached the road that descended the other side of the hill. The one that headed south, the direction his command would go when the word came, as it soon would. Three hours, more or less, from leaving camp, they would turn east, and cross the border to Spain perhaps an hour or so later.

He needed a clear head to lead his men, but his mind was a yawning shrieking storm of pain and anger. Perhaps he should send Dorothea home to England, to be dealt with later, when the war was over. He should have known her love was too good to be true. When had love ever worked out for him. *Never. I would have loved the earl, had he let me. But all the time he was lying to me. Stealing my name and my rights.* Grandda O'Toole had lied, too, and Maa and Papa. They would love him forever, they said. *But they died and abandoned me to England and the earl.*

In all his life, he had been the foreign one. The one who didn't fit. In India, the half-breed boy who was not Bengali or Irish or English. An officer's son who was also a sergeant's grandson. In England, the base-born son of a noble house—and one, furthermore, with tainted blood—foisted on aristocrats in the public school to which the earl had sent him, and later, on the officer's mess of the dragoons.

If not for Fox, he would have been entirely alone, facing bullying and scorn in both new environments.

But Fox stood his friend, and Lion could fight like a demon and ride as if born on horseback. At school, he excelled in all sports, and was soon known as both too dangerous to bully and a good man to have at one's side. In battle, he became a storm as the red rage that filled him drove his body, though years of practice meant he could usually keep some part of his mind detached and observant.

At school, he made friends. In the army, he won the respect of his colleagues and the admiration of his men.

Not their love. Their love was neither offered nor wanted, for soldiers die in war, and Lion suffered pain enough seeing those he ate with and fought beside submit one by one to the grim linked scythes of battle or disease.

Dorothea had made a fool of him. She had told him what he wanted to hear. He had given his heart and his trust. He had thought her true; one true woman out of all the silly females who had set out to seduce him over the years.

A notch on their beds, that was all he was to them. The earl's bastard grandson. Or the man whose Indian blood had given him erotic powers beyond English understanding. Or the hero of whatever battle was in the headlines at the time. They did not see him; only what he symbolised for them.

I believed Dorothea saw me!

Perhaps he was to blame as much as she. She had been desperate to avoid marriage to Westinghouse, and who could blame her? Women were so powerless. Wouldn't she say whatever she thought he wanted to hear in order to escape her fate? At least he could acquit her of marrying him for his title or the wealth that went with it, since he'd had neither when they wed.

On the other hand, Fox's suggestions of Brabant's hand in their marriage were unfortunately entirely possible. Though how could Brabant have known that Lion would stop at that inn? Or perhaps that was not the original plan, but an inspired improvisation. Anyone who had studied him would have known he could not resist helping her. He drew the line at thinking Lady Blaine in on the plot, but Mrs Austin had led his old friend's mother to them, and made their marriage inevitable.

Is that why Dorothea was so insistent on coming to Portugal to join him? But still, he found it hard to believe she was working with Westinghouse. Her loathing for the man was genuine, Lion would swear to it.

Perhaps the man Fox saw was not Westinghouse, but another. Not Michael, but someone who would betray her husband might take other lovers. He had married her in haste, and then abandoned her to return to his duty, leaving her with one attractive man after another. Fox was right about that, although he was wrong about her having lovers before Lion. Still, she had learned fast and she was a lusty wench. Even now, angry and grieved though he still was, he grew hard thinking of their coupling.

Though the thought of her with another man, with Michael Cassiday, whom he'd believed to be his friend, doused his lust quickly enough.

The sound of hooves behind him had him turning quickly, hand on his sword. It was Blythe, riding one horse and leading another.

"Messenger from General Picton, Colonel, sir. He is calling a meeting of his commanders."

A melia returned from her errand nervous and upset, but trying not to show it.

Bianca didn't notice. She was trying to decide what she would wear for her Anglican wedding. They had had trouble finding a Catholic priest who was willing to perform the wedding ceremony between her and her heretic beloved. And then Bianca had remembered her cousin Tomas, who was a priest in Guarda. She and Michael had gone to see him.

"You were right to urge me to tell him my story," she told Dorothea. "At first, he would not agree. I had to tell him what the French did to me and how Michael saved me and asked for nothing in return, but how my father turned me away and I came back to the camp with Michael because I had nowhere else to go. I told him we fell in love, and surely it is God's will that we be together, since I am a ruined woman but Michael loves me anyway."

She smiled through tears. "Father Tomas hugged Michael, gave us his blessing, and performed the ceremony on the spot."

On Wednesday, the chaplain would wed them again, this time for the piece of paper that would allow Bianca to return to England as Michael's wife.

Amelia declared her delight, and joined the other two women in searching through their combined wardrobes for something suitably bridal for the occasion.

Dorothea was wearing her husband's precious handkerchief against her skin, tucked into her stays so she could not possibly lose it again. How it got from her bedchamber to Michael's coat, where Bianca found it, neither she nor Bianca had been able to guess.

Perhaps it didn't matter. She had it, and when Lion returned, she would be able to show it to him and all would be well again.

Lion had ridden away without returning to the farmhouse. Fox had arrived just as Michael was leaving—apparently the general who would command them had called the senior officers of all his regiments to a meeting. "Not you, Cassiday," Fox had said. "Lion's orders. You are to remain. Officer-in-charge."

Michael's face had fallen, but he had gone off to check the sentries, and Fox had left with the others.

Still, Michael had been left in charge, which was a good sign, was it not? Didn't it mean that Lion had forgiven him for the fight? And when Lion saw that she had his mother's handkerchief back, he would forgive Dorothea, too.

The only cloud on her horizon was Amelia's distress. Several times, Dorothea looked up to see Amelia gazing at her, eyes welling with tears.

Her chance to find out what was wrong with her friend came when Michael returned and whisked Bianca into their bedchamber. "To discuss marriage," he said, with a twinkle in his eyes that said clearly what part of marriage and what sort of discussion he had in mind.

Dorothea drew Amelia into the bedchamber she shared with Lion, and firmly shut the door. "Amelia, whatever is the matter? Is it Fox?"

Amelia shook her head, tears running down her face. "Not Major Foxton. Colonel O'Toole. Lord Harcourt, I mean. He was so angry, my lady. Dorothea. I tried to tell him… but he told me I was lying!"

Bit by bit—for Amelia was very upset and kept drifting from a report on the conversation to her own emotions at Lion's accusations—Dorothea got the story out of her. At first, her mind rejected what she heard. Amelia must be mistaken. She must have misheard.

A lover? No. How could he think such a thing? It could not be true.

Her body knew, though. The hollow sickness in her abdomen,

the ache in her chest, the whirling of her head; all spoke to a gut-deep understanding of the reason for Lion's earlier anger. He truly believed she had betrayed him. For some reason, he thought the handkerchief was evidence.

But I have it back! As quickly as she had the thought, she dismissed its comfort. Lion would simply think she had asked this mythical lover for it.

Suddenly, she was furious. "I have done nothing to make him doubt me," she declared. "Nothing, Amelia." Indeed, she had done her best to support him in every way, and never to demand that he put her before his duty. *I will kill him. Or myself.* No. She wouldn't. She would fight with him until he listened to her, for their marriage was worth fighting for.

"I know it, Dorothea. I told him you did not have a lover. I told him you were with me all night. Me and Mrs Meadows."

"So why does he think I have been unfaithful?" Dorothea wondered.

Amelia sighed. "He is a man, Dorothea. He has had women before. Married women, as well as widows and harlots. I suppose he thinks it is what women do."

"It is not what I do," Dorothea declared. "Even if I did not love the man to distraction, I would never break my vows."

"Men do," Amelia said, with deep conviction. "Men are always unfaithful. They chase after any female who appeals to them, and never think of their wives."

Dorothea shook her head. "Not Lion," she said. "He loves me." *But if he truly loves me, he would not judge me and find me guilty without even checking his facts!*

"He is a man," Amelia repeated. "If he takes his pleasure with another, he will expect you to pretend you do not know, but if you do the same… It is terrible, Dorothea, but it is the way of men."

She frowned. "You must ask him who this imaginary lover is, and on what dates and times you have been with him, and then we will prove that it is all lies," she said.

She seemed to think she had been a comfort, but Dorothea felt worse, and not better. Lion was not the man she had thought him, and the knowledge had broken her.

Yes, she would plead her case. She had no choice. She was in Lion's power, which had never bothered her before, because he made her feel safe. But now she was afraid. Lion was not the man she thought him. She did not know if he could be trusted.

CHAPTER 16

Lion sent Fox and Bear ahead with the men and found a place to sit where he could overlook the camp.

In the course of the day, he had imagined wiping out the insult of her betrayal by killing her. Yes, and Michael Cassiday, too. Not that he was going to do it. He wouldn't go home until he was sure he was in control, but the longer he sat the less calm he felt.

Lion had visualised a bullet for Michael, or killing him with his own officer's sword. Not a duel. The kind of scum who took advantage of his colonel's wife did not deserve the honour of a duel. Fox had offered to execute the man for him, but Lion said he wanted the pleasure for himself.

Visualising was all he could do. An officer in His Majesty's cavalry could kill for the King, but not for his own private revenge.

As to his wife, he could not kill her, either. He could not use a gun on her. He could not bear to think of the damage that a bullet would do to the body he had loved with such passion and tenderness. The same applied to a knife.

He had considered strangling her with his own hands, but he couldn't do that, either. To touch her with violence—no, it was inconceivable. He could not see her suffer or mar the perfection of her skin in any way.

Perhaps he would remain here until morning, grieving over the wreck of his marriage and wondering how to find out for certain whether any of the three were also guilty of selling secrets to the French. Not Cassiday, surely. He would believe it of Westinghouse. As for Dorothea, it hurt too much to think about her.

A shape trudged up the hill towards him. "Colonel. Mind if I join you?"

It was the exploring officer known as Bull. The one who had been betrayed by the Greek spy. "Why do women do it?" Lion demanded.

Bull sat down on the rock beside him and stared out over the landscape. "I'm the last person you should ask about women, Colonel. Trouble in the dovecote?"

Lion's glare wiped the smirk off the man's face, but he didn't move. "It's bad, then. What do you think she did?"

"Spent last night with a lover. Gave him a gift I'd given her. Lied about it." Put baldly like that, it sounded wrong. That wasn't the Dorothea he knew.

Bull's eyes narrowed. "Last night? She and Mrs Foxton spent the whole night last night with Mrs Meadows. Woman had a healthy son. Word was all over the camp. The women won't be happy to think someone is telling tales about Mrs O'Toole. They regard her as some sort of saint."

Lion gazed at him, for a moment, his mind blank. "Where were Cassiday and Bianca last night?"

"That's the other news everyone is talking about. The lady has finally agreed to put the poor major out of his misery. She has a cousin who is a priest and was willing to marry them, and they'll get married again by our chaplain." He shrugged. "The cousin is a fair stretch away, in Guarda, and they ended up staying the night, but Mr and Mrs Cassiday are undoubtedly celebrating their honeymoon as we speak."

Lion was reeling. *If Michael and Bianca left together yesterday, then Fox lied about Bianca abandoning Michael, and probably the argument he claimed to have heard. If he lied about that…* Lion drew the obvious conclusion. If Fox had gone to so much trouble to make Dorothea seem guilty, then he must have had a reason. And what better reason than diverting attention from himself?

I should have known. Dorothea is true and good. "I am a fool, Bull," he admitted. "The man who told me… I don't trust him with money. He's a good soldier, but I haven't recommended him for promotion because I don't trust him to command anything more than a squadron. Why did I think he could be trusted with my wife's reputation?"

"Foxton?" Bull asked. "He shows you a different face than the rest of us see. Don't believe a word he says, Lion." The words shook Lion, not just because Bull had put an unerring finger on the culprit, but because of what he implied about Lion's blindness.

He stood. "Thank you, Bull. You've been a great help." He set off down the slope towards the farmhouse and Dorothea.

Dorothea lay sprawled on their bed, still fully dressed but sound asleep, though it was only early evening. Lion bent over her, and his heart turned over in his chest. Her eyes had the red puffy look of someone who had cried herself to sleep and the tracks of tears stained her cheeks.

As he gazed at her asleep, he realised that a pillow would have been a solution to the conundrum he'd been considering when Bull arrived. He could have placed it over her face and held it down. He wouldn't have had to look at her. Death would have been as kind as death ever could be in one so young.

He shuddered, and his tears were as much revulsion as grief and shame. He could never have done it. Surely, when it came to the point, he would have talked to her instead.

He placed a gentle hand on Dorothea's shoulder. "Dorothea. It's me. Lion."

She rolled towards him and nuzzled into his hand, still more asleep than awake. "Lion," she murmured, his name warm and welcoming on her lips. Then her eyes shot open and she drew away. Her smile dropped and she faced him with wary eyes. "Lion." This time, her voice was carefully neutral.

His aching heart sank. He had done that to her—broken her trust in him. He dropped to his knees beside the bed. "Dorothea, I am sorry. I was wrong. I was so wrong not to believe in you, not to listen to you." He needed her forgiveness more than he needed his next breath, but he had no right to it. He had hurt her—the woman he had sworn to protect with his life. How could he beg her pardon when what he had done was unpardonable?

"Why, Lion?" she asked. The question he had been struggling with all the way back into camp, since he realised that Fox had lied, lied, and lied again.

"I trusted the wrong person," he admitted. "Someone told me lies about you, then I saw something that seemed to confirm those lies." He shook his head. "It is no excuse. I should not have believed him. I did not, at first, but he kept saying things… It took me until now to understand that the person he described, the person who could do what he said, she wasn't you."

The hurt in her expression had not abated. "You should have known better."

Could she understand what he had only just realised? "Yes. And I did, eventually. I just never expected… The truth is that I don't deserve your love. I know that. I think I was waiting to find out it was all a mistake. I am too old for you, too battered by life."

She sat up, anger flashing in her eyes. "Nonsense, Lion. If anyone is undeserving, it is me. A merchant's daughter. No one in particular. Too old and too common for the marriage mart."

"We have had this discussion before," he realised.

"Yes. Let us not do it again." She reached out for his hands and he took hers, his heart suddenly lighter because she was willing to touch him. "You hurt me, Lion, because you didn't trust me. You believed the worst about me. Amelia told me you thought I had taken a lover. How could you, Lion?"

He clung to hope the way she was clinging to his hands. She was holding on to him. She was still talking to him. "Everyone who matters to me has left me," he explained. *That doesn't even make sense. They had no choice.* He could not blame them for dying.

"Your parents and your Grandfather O'Toole," she guessed, and he nodded. "And the friends I made when I first joined the regiment. All dead, now."

She pulled one hand from his grasp, but only to lay it alongside his face, cupping his cheek. "Lion, you make it very hard to stay angry with you."

Hope blossomed. "You ought to be angry with me."

Her chuckle was somewhat watery, for tears were flowing down her cheeks. "I am. But I love you, Lion. I thought you had broken my heart, but I find you are putting it back together again. Do not hurt me like that again. I could not bear it."

"I promise that, if ever I think I have reason to be upset with you, I will ask you for an explanation and listen to your answer," he told her. "And I will never again take someone else's word against yours."

"I promise the same," Dorothea said.

She leaned towards him in invitation, and he gladly took her lips. It was a kiss of forgiveness. One of homecoming and blessing. And when it began to heat into something different, he pulled reluctantly away. Not far, though. At some point in the kiss, he had climbed on the bed to be closer to her, and now he sat, his arm around her, his back against the wall and his legs stretched out beside hers.

"I need your help, my love. To catch the man who tried to tear us apart."

"Fox," Dorothea said. "It was Fox, wasn't it?"

"Yes, but how did you know? Has he been playing his tricks on you, too?"

Dorothea nodded. "Subtle tweaks and pinpricks, if that is what you mean. His theme is that I am unfit to be your wife, and you are bored with me and have returned to your other women. When you were so cold to me, I was afraid he was right. Amelia didn't help, though I think she was just trying to be helpful. She said I must expect you to be unfaithful because men are like that."

"Fox is," Lion acknowledged. "Not I, Dorothea. You are my wife, and I want no one else."

"Even if I go back to England and leave you here?" she asked.

His hope turned brown and withered. "That is your right," he acknowledged. "It is what I deserve. It is better than I deserve." And he would mourn her leaving, pine for her while they were apart, and do his best to win her back through letters. She was silent and still, her eyes solemn as she gazed at him.

She was waiting, he realised. "And no, I will not take a lover if you leave me. I will lie with no one else until we are together again."

It was the right answer. Colour bloomed in her face and she smiled.

"I am not going, you know. I am staying with the army and going where you go. I will not let that horrid man win. I know he is your cousin, Lion, but I do not like James Foxton. It was a terrible thing he tried to do."

"More than you know," Lion told her. "I think he might be our traitor; the man who has been selling secrets to the French." *And, incidentally trying to kill me.* He wouldn't mention that to Dorothea at the moment. That news would come better after Fox was captured and in prison.

From the other room, they could hear the quiet buzz of conversation. At least two of the other residents had arrived home.

"Will you help me lay a trap for him, my love?" Lion asked.

D orothea lay still on the bed, her limbs awkwardly sprawled, her eyes shut. She heard the squeak as the bedchamber door opened. Some practical part of her mind made a note to ask Blythe for some grease for the hinges.

Lion left the door partly open so she could hear. So far, nothing, but she knew what Lion was doing. He was sure that, if he really had killed her, he would have been out of his mind. "For I was well on the way to half-mad today, my love, and if I had not met Bull up on the hillside, I might be yet."

He would never have done it, he assured her. "I would have needed to be deranged, and even then, I cannot imagine laying angry hands on the body I have loved so much—but if I had, Dorothea, it would have driven me completely insane."

So now he was in the living room, pretending to be a lunatic. Exactly how, would depend on who was there. She strained her ears, hearing voices but not words. Amelia and Lion. No one else. Then Amelia, closer, saying, "I will just check on my lady. Colonel. Please sit down. You are not well."

The door squeaked, and Amelia screamed.

"I had to do it," Lion said, sadly. "I could not let anyone else hurt her. I loved her too much."

"Murder!" Amelia shrieked. "Murder! The Colonel has killed our lady! Murder!"

A clatter of boots and the patter of bare feet.

Fox's voice, then. "Lion. What have you done?"

"I had to do it," Lion repeated. "You know, Fox. You are the one that told me, that proved it to me. This is your fault, Michael. You should never have seduced my wife. Or did she seduce you?"

"You're mad," Michael said. "Your wife and I? Never."

"It is a lie," Bianca said, at the same time.

"Fox told me," Lion said. "He said you spent the night together last night, that she gave you the handkerchief that once belonged to my mother. And I saw Bianca hand it to you."

"No," Fox protested. "I said nothing of the kind. Why would I? Michael and Bianca were away last night. And I know nothing of any handkerchief."

"That is a lie," Amelia said, her voice shrill. "I told you about—"

"Be quiet, bitch," Fox demanded. "Do not interrupt your betters."

"Let her talk," Lion ordered.

Cassiday agreed. "Finish what you were saying, Amelia."

Dorothea allowed her eyes to open a crack, peering through her lashes. Cassiday was blocking the way out the door. He held a pistol, which he was currently pointing at Fox, though his wary glances at Lion indicated he had not yet caught on to their ruse.

Bianca stood at Cassiday's side, and Amelia was by the bed, her back to Dorothea.

"Go on, Mrs Foxton," Lion encouraged.

"I told Major Foxton about my lady's handkerchief," Amelia insisted, "and how she carried it with her always. I was collecting her clothes for laundering when he came to talk to me. I found the handkerchief in her pocket and I told him how much she loved it. He said it once belonged to the Colonel's mother. He said he would take it to my lady."

"How then, did it find its way into the pocket of Michael's great-coat?" Bianca asked, her eyes fixed on Fox.

"You bastard," Michael said to Fox.

"No. It is all a mistake," Fox insisted. "You can see who is at fault here. Lion has gone mad and killed his wife."

It was time. Dorothea sat up. "No, he is not. And he did not. You are a liar, Major Foxton. You set out to destroy my marriage. You worked on me and when I would not be frightened off, you tried to fool Lion into believing I had betrayed him. You lied to Lion, about Michael and the fight with Westinghouse. You told Lion that Westinghouse said something rude about Bianca, but I know what really happened. Michael rescued Bianca from Westinghouse's assault. I find myself asking what you told Westinghouse that made him feel he was safe attempting to rape a major's woman in a military camp."

Michael took a hasty step forward, the pistol pointed unerringly at Fox's abdomen. "You unmitigated swine."

Lion sounded tired when he said. "We lock him up, Michael, and we search his belongings." He raised his voice. "Gentlemen!" The tramp of boots answered his call as he said, "And if I am right, we will find reason enough to shoot him for the traitor he is."

"No!" Fox shrieked. "I am your friend, Lion. Your only friend in the world." Captain Gavenor and a couple of his men entered the room and one man took each of Fox's arms. He struggled, but they forced him out of the room.

"Michael, I want you and Bear to search. Amelia, I am sorry, but we will need to go through everything. Do you want to watch to make sure they do not damage anything of yours?"

But Amelia's mind had finally grasped the full horror of what had happened. She sank into a heap on the floor and burst into noisy sobs.

Bianca moved to her side, and Dorothea slid off the bed to her other side.

"Do what you must, Lion," she told him. "Bianca and I will look after Amelia."

They found nothing in Fox's room except a philtre of opium oil, which, Michael suggested, explained why he remembered nothing of the attack on Westinghouse. Fox continued to protest his innocence. Lion and Bear went to question him in the makeshift gaol they'd made out of what might once have been a woodshed.

He had changed his story a little. In the new version, he had seen how close Michael and Dorothea had become. "I must have misunderstood what Bianca said in the argument she had with Michael." A smile and a shrug. "She speaks so much Spanish when she gets excited."

Cue the sincere face. "When I was told Bianca had left and I discovered Michael missing from his room, I guessed Michael was with Dorothea. I gather now I was mistaken. I am so sorry, Lion. It was a genuine error, but a very hard one for you. I understand why you are angry."

Next came the bravely suppressed hurt. "But to suspect me of treason! Lion, come on! You will find nothing in my room because there is nothing."

"The colonel isn't taken in by your theatrics," Bear grumbled.

Fox directed a malevolent glance his way and then pasted a carefree smile over it. "I am not your traitor, Lion," he insisted.

Yes, he was. However, Lion didn't have enough evidence to take to a court martial. Anyone with half a brain could drive a coach and four through Fox's explanation, but Lion wouldn't put it past Fox to paper over the cracks with a large dollop of charm.

He returned dispirited to the farmhouse, where Dorothea greeted him with the words, "Amelia has something to tell you."

CHAPTER 17

"There was enough there to have him shot ten times over," Lion reported to Dorothea after they'd searched the two places Amelia had suggested they try. He and Dorothea were lying on the bed, Lion propped on the pillows and Dorothea in his arms.

"Not at the first place, but at the second."

The first was a sentry post on the outside fortifications of Almeida. It faced the camp, so they hadn't bothered manning the post, and Fox had put it to his own use. Amelia had explained, tears welling over, "The wife of the Prefeito meets him there. She is Fox's mistress. When we first camped here, there was the padeira, the baker, too. On different days. But they found out about one another and there was a huge fight."

Lion remembered the fuss at the time. The mayor's wife and the lady baker, pulling one another's hair, and scratching and kicking in the marketplace. Their husbands had had to drag them home, but this was the first Lion had heard of the reason.

"How do you know all this?" Lion had asked.

Dorothea, who had her arm around Amelia's shoulders, tightened the comforting grasp into a hug, and the poor woman looked as if she needed it. She drooped in her seat. Her eyes, swollen with crying, seemed to have lived a thousand years, and all of them full of grief and sorrow.

"The women in the camp," she explained. "Someone always sees what is going on, or hears it. The women don't tell their men, but they tell each other. And they tell me when the one who strays is Major Foxton. They were jealous when he married me, you see."

Lion and the searchers found plenty of evidence that someone was using the place as a love nest, and some of the clothing left behind might be incriminating if the charge was adultery. But not what he wanted.

The second place was upstream from the camp. Amelia had wept all through her description of how to find it. "It is where I used to meet Fox when he was courting me," she explained. Lion met Dorothea's eyes, and saw his own thoughts reflected in hers. *Seducing her, more like.*

Somehow, Fox had discovered a hut, or a half-hut half-cave, hidden in a bank just above the river. It was well concealed in the undergrowth, but there were signs for those who knew how to read them that the path was well used, and that brush had been pulled over to conceal it.

It was there they found what they needed.

"Notes for reports for the French. Instructions for information they wanted and the price they were prepared to pay for it," he told Dorothea. "From what I saw, he has been working with them for at least the last eighteen months." He shook his head, slowly. "I can't understand it. How could he do it, Dorothea?"

Dorothea found it impossible to comprehend. Fox had been setting up his own men, his friends, his cousin, to die at the hands of the French. For money! "I don't know, my love. He isn't the man you believed him to be."

Lion's next remark had her removing her head from his chest so she could see his expression. "He was behind Westinghouse coming to Portugal."

"He was? But why?"

Lion pulled her back into his arms. "To cause trouble, I suppose. Westinghouse wrote him a couple of letters. One to thank him for the money for passage and the letter of introduction to the conde, and one to tell him of the rumours Westinghouse had been spreading."

"He is a fiend," Dorothea said. "I know he is your cousin, Lion, but he is a horrid person."

"He is," Lion agreed. He stroked a hand over her hair and kissed the top of her head. "I am grieving the boy I once knew, Dorothea. He hasn't been that boy for a long time, but I didn't see it. Perhaps he never was what I thought. He always had a nasty tongue, and he thought being born a viscount's son and an earl's grandson made him better than nearly all the rest of the world. But he was kind to me, when I was a lonely boy."

"People can change when they grow up," Dorothea said. "Some for the better; some for the worse. He chose his own path, Lion. It is not your fault."

"And we caught him before he could do more harm." Lion sighed, but it was a sigh of relief. "He was upset when I kept using him as a courier instead of taking him to meetings with Picton, but he cannot have told the French any details of our invasion plan, because he didn't know any. The timing, of course, but any fool with a telescope knows we will be on the march soon."

Dorothea had more domestic concerns. "We will look after Amelia, will we not, Lion?"

He kissed her hair again. "Of course, we will. She is our cousin by marriage. We shall find out what she wishes to do, and we will make it happen. Dorothea, I have to go and question Fox about what we found."

She moved off his chest and slid out of bed. "Of course. Lion, you are not responsible for your cousin's behaviour, though he will try to make it all your fault. He could have stopped gambling at any time. He did not need to have so many lovers, all requiring gifts. He made bad choices, Lion. You have made good ones."

He came around the bed to embrace her. "I am holding one of the best choices I ever made," he told her.

D orothea was right. Once Fox discovered they had found his cache of documents, he first railed against Amelia then tried to cast all the blame onto Lion.

Lion sat stoically through a tirade about the misbegotten bastard who had always got in his way. The base-born scoundrel who had stolen Fox's grandfather's affection, outdone Fox at sport and school-work, and progressed more quickly through the ranks. The despicable by-blow who used his power not to help his cousin but to promote other less worthy people and who forced Fox to marry a stupid chit with no money and no breeding.

Lion's unwanted title came in for its share of vituperation. Fox seemed to take it as a purposeful insult that the bastard had turned out to be legitimate and the heir. But what had driven Fox to such extremes, in Fox's view, was Lion's meanness with money; his refusal to help Fox out.

By which, Lion took it, Fox meant Lion had refused to give his cousin crippling amounts of money in loans that would never be repaid.

"Enough," he said at last. "We have all the evidence we need to put before a court martial, Fox. You will have your chance to present counter evidence. I have sent a message to the general, and I will let you know a date and time when I have them."

He walked out to a stream of curses.

Blythe met him partway across the camp. "The Conde de Estombar is here, colonel. He begs for a minute of your time."

What now? "Were those his words, corporal? He begs a minute of my time?" Astoundingly polite, after their previous interactions.

"Yes, sir," Blythe confirmed. "He is with Lady Harcourt at your house, sir."

"Is Westinghouse with him?" Lion prepared to run.

"No, sir. Just servants. He left them outside with his carriage.

The conde in a peasant farmhouse? With Dorothea left to be his hostess without Lion's support? He hastened his steps.

He need not have worried, he decided. Dorothea was equal to anything. The nobreza was in the living room's most comfortable chair, enjoying a glass of their best port, with a plate of cheese and dried fruit within reach.

He, Dorothea, and Bianca appeared to be enjoying a comfortable chat. Amelia was nowhere to be seen. The conde stood up when he entered. "Lord Harcourt. I give you greetings."

Lion knew the gentlemanly forms. "Senhor Conde. You honour my humble house. I am sorry I was not at home to receive you."

A lift of one elegant shoulder. "Your delightful wife and Senhora Cassiday have made me very comfortable. May I speak with you in private, Lord Harcourt? I will not take much of your time."

"Perhaps you and Dom de Estombar would like to take your wine out to the bench, my lord?" Dorothea suggested. She was pouring him a glass as she spoke.

The conde inclined his head, and led the way, carrying his glass. Lion took the glass Dorothea offered him, mimed a kiss, and picked up the plate of edibles before following the older gentleman outside.

They took the bench against the wall, and Lion waited for his visitor to disclose his errand.

It did not take long. The conde took a fortifying sip of his port and then said, "I was raised to think it rude to speak of business straight away, but I know you British have different customs, so I hope you will forgive me for immediately explaining my visit."

Lion, who was burning with curiosity, tried to sound indifferent. "Of course, sir. I am at your service."

"I have come to offer an apology for my support of my erstwhile guest and to warn you of a cobra escondida—you would say a hidden snake, I think. Senhor Westinghouse showed his true colours when he insulted the daughter of a member of my household." The nobreza's eyes were implacable as he continued, "Sadly, he accidently fell during the ensuing discussion with my cavalheiro. He hit his head and nothing could be done for him. My servants packed up his belongings to send to his family, and they came across these letters, which they brought to me."

The conde felt inside his coat to extract and hand over a

package of letters addressed to R. Westinghouse. Lion knew the hand in which they were inscribed. Fox had written these. "You have my thanks, conde. My wife and Mrs Cassiday will be relieved that other women are now safe from the villain. As to the villain at my end, we have him imprisoned for other crimes, but these letters might help to seal his fate at his court martial."

That fetched him a faint smile. "Ah, the British. The legal process, you call it, yes? It is, I grant you, a civilised way to behave. In this case, however, I am pleased to have been able to make my own rules."

Which begged the question of how Westinghouse fell, and how far. Lion was not going to ask. Best for international relations if it was put down as a tragic accident.

"It is a very fine porto you have here, Lord Harcourt," the nobreza commented. "Almost as good as those from my own cellars. Perhaps you would permit me to send you a few bottles? A gesture of friendship, and of appreciation for the hospitality of your lovely wife. I am pleased to have had the chance of conversation with her. No doubt you have much to do, and I do not wish to take up too much of your time." He made no move to get up though, but sat relaxed on the bench, sipping his port.

"These moments of peace in the midst of war are necessary, sir," Lion said. "To sit in the sun, with an excellent wine, a tasty cheese, and pleasant company; such moments remind us of what we fight for. To make the simple pleasures something we can enjoy every day, not just a brief interlude in the midst of chaos. I am glad you came."

The conde smiled again, this time more broadly. They sat in a companionable silence. When the conde finished his glass, he stood. "I will take my leave, Lord Harcourt. My compliments to your wife. I hope we shall have the opportunity to meet again, in more peaceful times."

With a few more effusive compliments on both sides, Lion saw the nobreza to his coach, and bowed his goodbyes. As the coach began to move, the conde looked past Lion and his lips curved in appreciation. He blew a kiss of farewell to Dorothea, who was waving from the doorway. The coach rolled away, and Dorothea held out her hand to Lion.

"Blythe," Lion called, as he walked towards her.

The corporal appeared from around the side of the house. "Yes, sir?"

"Take these to Captain Gavenor. Tell him they are letters from Foxton to Westinghouse, and will be needed for the court-martial." He handed the package over without taking his eyes off Dorothea.

As Blythe raced away through the camp, Lion allowed Dorothea to tug him through the living room and into their bedchamber. "Do you have more meetings or other work in the next hour, Lion?" she asked, the husky note in her voice further inflaming his desire which had stirred, as always, at her touch.

"Not for the rest of the day, my love," he decided. "Why don't I lock the door, and you can show me what you want of me."

Another simple pleasure to drive back chaos, and this one within his reach as Dorothea came into his arms. She was home. She was peace. She was the symbol of everything he fought for.

EPILOGUE

Ruthford House, London, June 1815

By the second week of June, Lion could no longer wait in Persham Abbey. A great battle seemed inevitable when Napoleon confronted the forces massing against him in the Low Countries, and news would be sent to London, before anywhere else. He had to be there.

Dorothea was certainly not going to be left behind. Lion would need her as he waited for news of the men he still regarded as his. He had resigned his commission fourteen months ago, when Napoleon's surrender was in sight, the victory of the British and their allies inevitable. Dorothea had been heavy with child and Lion's great aunt had written to say the old earl was not long for this world.

Dorothea had done her best to reassure Lion, who worried that —because he was large and she was very little—the birth might be difficult. Amelia told him bluntly that Dorothea might be short, but she had wide hips. Lady Blaine growled at him for fussing. In the end, Dorothea gave birth with relative ease, forgetting the struggle as soon as her baby was placed in her arms.

Lion's grandfather lived long enough for them to bring him his new-born greatgrandchild, just a few hours old. With great effort, he moved a hand to touch her soft cheek. "Blessing," he said. Whether a wish, a benediction or a description, nobody in the room could say. His hand fell and his eyes closed, but his lips curved in a smile. Before Kathleen Patricia Benedicta Strathford-Bowes was six hours old, her great grandfather had died, and the little girl became Lady Kathleen, first child of the Earl and Countess of Ruthford.

Katie was now thirteen months old, and had been fully weaned for over a month—or had, in fact, weaned herself, clamping her mouth shut, new teeth and all, every time Dorothea offered her the breast. She had Nanny, a team of nursemaids, and her Aunt Patricia to dote on her, and an entire household whose activities revolved around her pleasures. She would miss her mother and father, no doubt, and be pleased to see them when they returned, but her loving attendants would coax her out of any dismals and distract her with walks and toys and games.

They had left Mr and Mrs Blythe in charge of the household. Amelia had married Blythe after a brief courtship. Being a widow in an army camp was a temptation and a distraction to the men, even a woman who was protected by the colonel. But Blythe admitted that he had loved Amelia for a long time, even before she was seduced by Fox, and Amelia's gratitude to him had turned to love before they returned to England with Lion and Dorothea. Blythe was now their butler, and Amelia their housekeeper and still Dorothea's friend.

Dorothea was aching to be with Katie again before Persham Abbey was out of sight. Lion, too, admitted to missing her. At home, he began every day with a visit to the nursery, and dressed early for dinner every evening so he could read Katie a story before she was put to bed.

On their first night in London, Lion had his own ideas about how to coax Dorrie out of the dismals, and himself, too. He had been calling her Dorrie since the first time she shortened Kathleen's name to Katie. It was his private name for her when they were alone, and being alone was precisely what he had in mind just now. His passion for her and hers for him had not faded in the two years since their marriage. Indeed, the weeks of forced celibacy after childbirth had made them treasure one another even more.

"I will admit to being pleased I don't share these any more, Dorrie, my love," Lion said, as he devoted himself to pleasuring first one breast and then the other.

"Until next time," Dorothea teased.

"We should work on next time," her husband proposed.

"I suppose we shall attend a few dinners and so on while we are in London?" Dorothea commented. Not that she felt like it. It seemed wrong to attend balls and other entertainments when people they knew were being wounded, even dying. Though some part of her wanted to flaunt her handsome earl in front of all the harpies and rakes who had made her London seasons a misery.

"Dinners!" Lion growled. "You have broken the rule that we do not speak of unpleasant things in our bed, and for that you must be punished."

In their bed, neither a loved and much-missed child nor a battle that would shape the future of Europe could be allowed to disturb the love that had only grown since those early days in Portugal.

Dorothea's punishment was being brought almost to her peak as many times as Lion could bear, before he broke and had to be inside her. Dorothea would have apologised for her lapse, but as her husband's fingers and mouth moved, she lost the ability to form coherent sentences.

The following day, however, they went out on afternoon calls and then on to dinner at the house of an old friend of Lion's from school, the Earl of Ashbury, whose wife was a daughter of a duke. Dorothea had become accustomed to being the highest-ranked lady in the room in her own small corner of Durham, but was a little nervous about the yawning gap between her pedigree and that of her hostess.

She needn't have worried. She was soon on first name terms with Val and Ruth Ashbury, and with Earl and Countess of Sutton, James and Sophia. James was Ruth's brother and heir to the Duke of Winshire, and Sophia was apparently related to, or at least acquainted with, the entire ton.

Indeed, many around the table were related to the host and hostess, and those who were not were equally pleasant.

The talk around the table was all about the rumours that Napoleon was marching on Brussels, where Wellington and other allied leaders were waiting for him. One man ventured the opinion that Wellington might lose, since he had never gone up against Napoleon himself.

One of the numerous ex-soldiers around the table made a rude noise, then blushed and apologised to the ladies. Another took it upon himself to explain to the heretic that Wellington would wipe the floor with Napoleon.

"It will not be an easy victory, though," said Val, which cast a dour spell over the whole table. Dorothea knew that Lion had been very tempted to do what their friends Bear Gavenor and Bull Moriarty had done, and reinlist when they first heard that Napoleon had escaped from Elba and that the French soldiers were flocking to march once more under his banner. Clearly, their host felt the same, though he had lost an arm to the wars and would not have been accepted even if he had volunteered.

Nods and glum looks from most of the other men showed that the sentiment was shared.

"We shall speak of our children," Ruth decreed. "Dorothea, I understand you have a little daughter. Is she with you in London?"

The other ladies followed her example, and soon the fond fathers joined in. When the ladies stood to leave the table, Dorothea was one of the last to quit the room, and so she heard one of the gentlemen suggest that now they could return to the subject of the war. "Women have no appetite for fighting, as is proper," he announced.

Lion disagreed. "Our children, gentlemen, are very much part of the same conversation, or there is no point in the battle. Unless we have peace and all its benefits clearly in our minds, what we bring back from war is chaos, and our wives and children are wise to remind us that the things of peace are and must be of far more significance in our lives than the evils we must do to defend them."

"Hear, hear," said Ashbury, and a chorus of other voices.

By the next day, rumours that battle had been joined were swirling around London. Lion went out in the morning to see what he could find out, but no one knew anything concrete.

"I don't know how many people I spoke to who are convinced the Corsican monster is even now on his way to England having massacred the largest army the allied forces have ever put into a single field," he told Dorothea, disgusted. "You will be pleased to know that I punched none of their stupid faces."

By that evening, the rumour was that there had been a great battle, a retreat, and a defeat. It was now the twentieth of June. The more credible reports suggested the French had crossed the northern border of France some five days ago, and engaged the Prussians, who had fallen back.

"Not a defeat," Lion scoffed, and the veterans among their friends agreed. "A fighting retreat until they can gather their numbers. If the Prussians were the only troops involved, it wasn't the main battle."

As Lion and Dorothea drove back to their townhouse, the streets were thronged with people waiting for official news.

The following morning, several of the London newspapers claimed that a bloody battle had been fought and won. But they provided no detail and ascribed the news to a gentleman who had arrived in London from Brussels. And a couple of them even said there may have been not a victory, but a defeat.

The couple kept themselves busy, but dread and hope mingled as they waited. "Even if the battle is over," Lion pointed out, "that doesn't mean the war is won."

Lady Sutton and her mother-in-law, the Duchess of Winshire, were holding a ball that night. Lion and Dorothea decided to go, rather than sit around their townhouse and fret about the outcome of the battle. "We will dance and talk with our friends, even as we pray for our comrades," Dorothea said.

It was close to midnight when the Duke of Winshire suddenly

halted the orchestra, and called out in a battlefield roar, "Listen! Outside! Do you hear?"

In the silence, the shouts of a crowd carried clearly through the French doors that were open all along one side of the ballroom. As one, the ball-goers surged for those doors, the closest reaching the terrace first and joining the shouting. "Victory! Hurrah!"

The orchestra struck up again, this time to the tune, God Save the King. Lion could feel tears prick his eyes. It was over, then.

He found Dorothea's hand. "It remains only to count the cost," he said. How many of his men had survived? Had Bear and the exploring officers? Had Michael? And what of Bianca?

Tears were running freely down Dorothea's cheeks, but she shook her head. "What remains is to safeguard and savour the peace," she replied.

He smiled down at the miracle who was his wife. "You are right, of course."

She showed that her thoughts had tracked with his when she added, "I wonder how long it will be before we know about our men?"

Lion shook his head, remembering the chaos that followed battle. And from what the papers had said so far, this had been beyond anything he had ever seen. "Some time, I would think."

"We will be there for them," Dorothea said, with a determined nod. "Whatever they need, whatever we are able to do. Our men will always be able to count on us."

How he loved this woman.

"They shall," he agreed. "But tonight is for celebration. Let us go home, my darling Dorrie. I have a more private celebration in mind."

"Home," Dorothea said. "Let us order the carriages for the morning, catch a few hours sleep, and go home to Katie and the north."

Footmen were streaming into the ballroom with trays of champagne. Lion caught two of the glasses as they passed, and handed one of them to his wife. "To Katie and the north," he said, and she raised her own glass to echo his toast and add to it. "To Katie and the families of all our comrades. To happy homecomings. To peace in our days. May God bless us all."

"He has," Lion told her. He took her glass from her hand and put both glasses on a passing tray. He led her from the ballroom, stopping only to make their farewells to Lady Sutton, who was by the door.

As they waited on the front steps for their carriage to be brought from the mews, he added, "He blessed me the day I found a stow-away in my luggage box. You *are* my comrade, my homecoming, my peace. You and Katie."

She stood on tiptoes to kiss him, ignoring the others who were waiting on the steps for their carriages.

She heard someone say, "How shocking," and someone else reply, "It is the Harcourts, dear. They were a love match. I think it is rather wonderful. And the man was a soldier. Surely tonight, such expressions of joy should be forgiven?"

Dorothea ignored them both. As their carriage rolled up in front of them, and Lion swept her into his arms to lift her into the carriage, she said, "And you are mine, Lion. My comrade. The home of my heart. My joy and my love."

For the sake of the sensibilities of the ladies on the steps, it was as well the footman closed the door at that moment. For Lion's answer to his wife's declaration was not in words, and would certainly have exceeded the tolerance even of the lady who sympathised.

As for Dorothea and Lion, they were far too busy to care.

THE END

AUTHOR'S NOTES

THE BRITISH ARMY IN PORTUGAL IN 1813

In November 1812, at the end of a long and relatively successful summer campaign in Spain, the British and their allies withdrew to go into winter quarters. During 1812, they had ejected the French from Ciudad Rodrigo, Badajoz, Seville, Astorga, and the provinces of Andalusia, Extremadura, and Asturias.

Wellington made his winter quarters just across the border from Ciudad Rodrigo, in Freineda, Portugal. I settled Lion's troops several hours ride north in Almeida, only later discovering that Almeida was a fortified village with its own Peninsular War story, which I've briefly mentioned in the novel.

The point of winter quarters was that sustained fighting in winter was well-nigh impossible. This is still true today. How much more so when moving the army relied on horses and mules, which consumed huge amounts of feed, and carts, which bogged down in the mud. And when armaments wouldn't work if the gunpowder got wet. During winter campaigns, troops died of the cold, of starvation, of exhaustion, of drowning during an attempt to cross rivers. Indeed, during Wellington's November retreat in 1812, hundreds of men died of exposure or hunger when a supply train was misdirected.

The Spring campaign in 1813 got off to a slow start for a couple of reasons. One was that dry weather meant little spring growth to sustain the horses and mules. The other was that river crossings relied on pontoons, and those Wellington had ordered in January were late arriving.

The Marquess of Wellington, as he was in 1813, is one of the two historical figures I've included in this book. General Picton is the other. It is a fact that he went home to England and returned in time for the summer offensive. His dealings with Lion are, of course, entirely invented, but consistent with the impression I've formed of him during my reading.

EXPLORING OFFICERS

Wellington had 'exploring officers', who would have challenged you to a duel had you dared to call them spies. They were officers and gentlemen, and if they did creep behind enemy lines to collect information, they wore their uniforms to do so. Wearing a disguise, lying about their name or identity, or other forms of deception would be beneath their code of civilised behaviour.

But Wellington (and other military leaders) also had other intelligence gatherers who were less particular. Did some of them include members of the great aristocratic families of England? If so, we would not expect to find out from the records. Such a secret would reflect badly on those families, and would never be disclosed.

My exploring officers and their men are, many of them, from the lower classes, and therefore not burdened with such niceties. I can imagine that Bear Gavenor would have worn his uniform at all times. Bull and Max would have done whatever was most likely to get the job done.

CIVILIANS AND THE ARMY

To our modern minds, it seems strange to think of civilians, including women and children, travelling into combat zones. Yet until the second half of the nineteenth century, civilians were an essential part of how armies worked. Collectively, anyone who followed the army that was not a soldier was called a camp follower. And every army had all kinds of followers.

All non-military supplies came from the commissariat, a civilian service, funded by Treasury. They searched for supplies, found a depot in which to store them, and staffed the depot and those who drove the mule carts that brought supplies in and out. Each local group of soldiers probably had a sutler, either semi-official or unsanctioned.

Sutlers negotiated with locals and sold goods that were not supplied by the commissariat: tobacco, coffee, sugar, and other supplies. A sutler was usually authorised at brigade level, and the role in each brigade often went to the wife of one of the soldiers.

Saddlers, tailors, shoemakers, and farriers might be soldiers (if someone with the right skills could be found) or civilians, but they were all essential to the operation of the army.

So were medical staff. The Army Medical Department employed around one surgeon for every 250 soldiers. Military surgeons were not commissioned into the army, so were technically civilians, but they were on the payroll. They were assisted by soldiers with more or less medical training, gained on the job, and by camp followers, usually wives of soldiers.

Wives and families formed the largest group of camp followers. In England, soldiers' families lived around the barracks, as military families do today. When the regiment travelled overseas, regulations stated how many wives they'd take with them (one for every six soldiers was common). To be in the ballot, a woman had to be a wife of good reputation. Mostly, women with children were excluded. On long overseas postings, babies arrived anyway, often on the march or even during battles.

Those not selected could seldom afford to follow their menfolk. They stayed in England and survived the best they could, often in a garrison city far from family, lacking work opportunities and not recognised as part of the local parish for poor relief.

Those selected faced hard work and unknown risks, but—though they might not be an official part of the army—they were on the books. Yes, they had to have an officer's approval to follow the army and they were subject to military discipline, but they received rations (a half ration for a wife and a quarter ration for a child) and they were paid for the work they did.

Wives were not only sutlers and nurses. They were also responsible for many other important jobs that kept the army operating: laundering clothes, cooking food, sewing and mending, watching the baggage, looking after sheep and cattle (food on the hoof), and acting as servants to officers and their families.

And, of course, they provided sexual services to their husbands. The rest of the soldiers in the unit would have to make other arrangements or go without. Wives who followed the army were, as I said before, women of good reputation.

Local women filled the gap, either on a temporary basis, as prostitutes, or longer term as mistresses or even wives. Locally acquired wives and families provided the same wide range of services as those brought overseas with the regiment, but the army didn't hold itself accountable for paying them or for transporting women and their children to England when the war was over, or when the soldier died, unless the woman could produce proof of a legal marriage, recognised by the Church of England.

As to the marriage of officers, the army discouraged young officers from taking a wife. Not only was it likely to ruin them financially, given the cost of being an officer—commission, uniforms, equipment, subscription, and the officers' mess. Marriage was thought to disturb the camaraderie of the mess, as it took the officer out of the all-male brotherhood of warriors.

A young officer who married without permission risked ruining his chances of promotion.

That changed as he went up through the ranks. An old rhyme said:

"A Subaltern may not marry,
    captains might marry,
    majors should marry,
    and lieutenant-colonels must marry."

HOW THE GOOD NEWS WAS BROUGHT FROM WATERLOO TO LONDON

In an age of instant news, when every war attracts both foreign correspondents and citizen journalists, it is hard for us to appreciate the atmosphere in London in the second half of June 1815.

Journalism as we know it had not yet been born, though London had scores of papers. Indeed, the news they printed came from reports from ordinary civilians who happened to know something, official reports printed verbatim, or articles lifted from other papers.

No one in London on 18th June 1815 knew that the great battle had taken place, let alone who had won. The news was slow to arrive, too. The battle was on a Sunday, and it wasn't until late on Wednesday that Wellington's messenger, Major Henry Percy, arrived in London, with a French eagle sticking out of each window of his yellow post chaise.

Escorted by a delirious crowd, he brought the report to Cabinet, who were dining in Grosvenor Square. After they'd read it and made an announcement to the crowd, Percy continued on, with an even larger crowd and followed by most of the Cabinet, to the house of a banking family where the Prince Regent was dining that night.

He must have had a flair for the dramatic, for he laid the eagles at the prince's feet, saying, "Victory, Sir, Victory."

REGENCY BOOKS BY JUDE KNIGHT

LION'S ZOO

A series about officers from an elite cadre of exploring officers returning to England and find love and danger.

Chaos Come Again, THIS BOOK

Grasp the Thorn, PUBLICATION IN JULY 2023
An accident brought Bear Gavenor and Rosa Neatham together. Scandal may tear them apart. (First published as *House of Thorns*.)

One Hour in Freedom, PUBLICATION IN NOVEMBER 2023

The Darkness Within, PUBLICATION IN DECEMBER 2023

A TWIST UPON A REGENCY TALE

Fairy tales (loosely) reinterpreted as Regency romances, but with magical elements transformed into natural happenings and the role of hero and heroine reversed.

Lady Beast's Bridegroom (Book 1 in *A Twist Upon a Regency Tale*)
Is the love of Beauty and his Lady Beast strong enough to overcome prejudice, hatred, and rejection?

The Talons of a Lyon (Part of the Lyon's Den Connected World)
Lance promised Mrs Dove Lyon he would take Lady Frogmore from Pond Street into High Society. Her nasty relatives are determined he will fail.
PUBLISHED APRIL 2023

One Perfect Dance (Book 2 in *A Twist Upon a Regency Tale*)

For sixteen years, Ash has owed Regina a dance. His step-brothers will do anything to keep him from the ball.

PUBLISHED MAY 2023

Snowy and the Seven Doves (Book 3 in *A Twist Upon a Regency Tale*)

The hero raised in a brothel. The heroine born to wealth and title. The villain who wants to destroy the first and own the second.

PUBLISHED AUGUST 2023

Crossing the Lyon (a novella in Night of Lyons)

The golden tickets are a trap for two innocent maidens. But who will the trap catch?

PUBLISHED AUGUST 2023

Perchance to Dream (Book 4 in A Twist Upon a Regency Tale)

Scared by life, they have abandoned dreams of romance. Until love's kiss awakens them.

PUBLISHED SEPTEMBER 2023

THE GOLDEN REDEPENNINGS SERIES

True love is rare and elusive, but they won't settle for less

Candle's Christmas Chair (A novella in *The Golden Redepennings* series)
They are separated by social standing and malicious lies. He has until Christmas to convince her to give their love another chance.

Gingerbread Bride (A novella in *The Golden Redepennings* series)
Mary runs from an unwanted marriage and finds adventure, danger and her girlhood hero, coming once more to her rescue.

Farewell to Kindness (Book 1 in *The Golden Redepennings* series)
Love is not always convenient. Anne and Rede have different goals, but when their enemies join forces, so must they.

A Raging Madness (Book 2 in *The Golden Redepennings* series)
Their marriage is a fiction. Their enemies are all too real. Uncovering the truth will need all the trust Ella and Alex can find.

The Realm of Silence (Book 3 in *The Golden Redepennings* series)
Rescue her daughter, destroy her dragons, defeat his demons, return to his lonely life. How hard can it be?

Unkept Promises (Book 4 in *The Golden Redepennings* series)

Mia hopes to negotiate a comfortable marriage. Jules wants his wife to return to England, where she belongs. Love confounds them both.

The Flavour of Our Deeds (Book 5 in The Golden Redepenning series)

When Luke finally admits to loving Kitty, she thinks their troubles are over. They are just beginning.

PUBLISHED IN MARCH 2023

The Golden Redepennings: Books 1 to 4

THE FIRST FOUR BOOKS OF THE SERIES ARE NOW AVAILABLE IN BOX SET FORM

THE RETURN OF THE MOUNTAIN KING

In 1812, high Society is rocked when the heir to the Duke of Winshire, long thought dead, returns to England with the children of his Persian-born wife and fierce armed retainers.

To Wed a Proper Lady: The Bluestocking and the Barbarian (Book 1 in The Return of the Mountain King series)

Everyone knows James needs a bride with impeccable blood lines. He needs Sophia's love more.

To Mend the Broken-Hearted: The Healer and the Hermit (Book 2 in The Return of the Mountain King series)

A woman doctor from a foreign land and a recluse earl with a missing hand find common ground nursing the children he loves, whether they are his or not.

Melting Matilda (A novella in the Return of the Mountain King series)

Sparks flew a year ago when the Granite Earl kissed the Ice Princess. In the depths of another winter, fire still smoulders under the frost between them.

To Claim the Long-Lost Lover: The Diamond and the Doctor (Book 3 in The Return of the Mountain King series)

The beauty known as the Winderfield Diamond hides a ruinous secret. Society's newest viscount holds the key.

To Tame the Wild Rake: The Saint and the Sinner (Book 4 in The Return of the Mountain King series)

The whole world knows Aldridge is a wicked sinner. The ton has labelled Charlotte a saint for her virtue and good works. Appearances can be deceptive.

Paradise Triptych (A collection in The Return of the Mountain King series)

Long ago, when they were young, James and Eleanor were deeply in love. But their families tore them apart and they went on to marry other people. This set of two novellas and a set of memoirs tells their story.

OTHER NOVELS

A Baron for Becky

She was a fallen woman. How could the men who loved her help set her back on her feet?

Revealed in Mist

As spy and enquiry agent, Prue and David worked to uncover secrets, while hiding a few of their own.

House of Thorns

His rose thief bride comes with a scandal that threatens to tear them apart.

OTHER NOVELLAS

The Husband Gamble

When the pawn becomes Queen, she and the opposing King will both win the game of love.

Lord Calne's Christmas Ruby

One wealthy merchant's heiress with an aversion to fortune hunters. One an impoverished earl with a twisted hand. Combine and stir with one villainous rector.

A Suitable Husband

A chef from the slums, however talented, is no fit mate for the cousin of a duke, however distant. But Cedrica can dream.

The Beast Next Door (A novella in the Bluestocking Belles collection *Valentines from Bath*)

In all the assemblies and parties, no-one Charis met could ever match the beast next door.

A Dream Come True (A novella in the Bluestocking Belles collection
Storm & Shelter)

The tempest that batters Barnaby Somerville's village is the
latest but not the least of his challenges. He does not expect the
storm that will batter his heart.

Lord Cuckoo Comes Home (A novella in the Bluestocking Belles
collection *Desperate Daughters*)

Two people who have never fitted in just might be a perfect fit.

LUNCH-LENGTH READS: STORY COLLECTIONS

Hand-Turned Tales and Lost in the Tale

A double handful of short stories and novellas, free from most
eretailers. Try the range of Jude's imagination one bite at a time, in
a lunch-length read.

If Mistletoe Could Tell Tales

A repackaging of six published Christmas stories: four novellas
and two novelettes. Because nothing enhances the magic of
Christmas like the magic of love.

Hearts in the Land of Ferns

Five stories all set in New Zealand: two historical and three contemporary suspense. All That Glisters has been published in Hand-Turned Tales. The other four have all been published in multi-author collections, but never before in a collection of Jude Knight stories.

Chasing the Tale and Chasing the Tale: Volume II
Short stories just long enough for a lunch or coffee break. In volume 1: Nine Regency plus one colonial New Zealand and one medieval Scotland. In volume 2: mostly Regency, with one Victorian New Zealand. Multiple tropes, catastrophes and barriers on the way to a happy ending.